**Date: 12/21/16**

# Dirty Sexy Saint

*NEW YORK TIMES BESTSELLING AUTHORS*

## Carly Phillips

## Erika Wilde

dirty SEXY
SERIES

CARLYPHILLIPS.COM
ERIKAWILDE.COM

**"Steamy, sexy and emotionally charged."**
**—J. Kenner, NY Times Bestselling Author of the Stark Series**

New York Times bestselling authors Carly Phillips and Erika Wilde bring you a dirty, sexy, smoking hot series featuring three bad boy brothers bonded by shocking secrets and their damaged past. Sinful, addicting, and unapologetically alpha, these men are every woman's erotic daydream ... And your ultimate dirty fantasy.

Are you ready to get Dirty Sexy with a Saint?

Clay Kincaid knows he's more a sinner than a saint. Especially when it comes to women. With a rough and damaged past that has left him jaded, he doesn't do committed relationships. But he does like sex—the hotter and harder, the better. He likes it fast and filthy, which is why he refuses to even touch someone as sweet and guileless as Samantha Jamieson. Until he discovers that she likes it just as down and dirty as he does. Let the sinning begin . . .

\* \* \*

# Chapter One

"I THINK IT'S time you proposed to my daughter, Harrison."

Samantha Jamieson stopped short of knocking on the door leading into her father's study as Conrad Jamieson's matter-of-fact statement made her heart jolt hard in her chest. She'd been dating Harrison Blackwell III for the past eight months, but recently she'd thought more about ending their relationship, not *marrying* him. Apparently her father had other ideas, and Samantha remained rooted to the spot just outside the room.

"I know it might feel like I'm rushing things along," Conrad went on in his deep, commanding voice, "but you've proven yourself as a top-level executive, and it's time to move you into the CEO position. Marrying Samantha would accomplish that goal, and will also ensure that the company stays in the family."

"Conrad, I'm honored you think of me that way," Harrison replied evenly, in that unemotional way he had about him. "In fact, I'd hoped this would be the end result of my time with Samantha."

Disgust rose in her throat as she realized that Harrison's determined pursuit was all for the sake of the firm and securing his position within the company. It had nothing to do with any romantic interest in her. She was a business transaction to both men and nothing more. And even if she'd contemplated breaking up with him, she'd been in the relationship for honest reasons. He, clearly, had not.

Her father's company, Jamieson Global, was a hedge fund enterprise and major investment firm, originally founded by Samantha's grandfather, who'd passed away of a heart attack over ten years ago. Her father had taken over the reins, and with Samantha as an only child and having no interest in any aspect of the family business, Conrad had obviously decided to set up an arranged marriage to a man who'd come from an equally wealthy and powerful family.

The arrangement between her father and Harrison shouldn't have surprised Samantha. All her life, she'd been well aware that her parents were grooming her for this position—from attending an exclusive all-girls academy to making certain she was well trained in handling herself in high-society situations. And for the most part, she'd been the quintessential good girl— obedient and respecting her parents' wishes for the past twenty-six years of her life while squashing the side of her personality that wanted to rebel against being molded into a perfect Stepford wife. That rebellion was scratching its way to the surface fast and furiously now.

She leaned against the wall and swallowed back a pained laugh as her father and Harrison continued to discuss her as if she were a commodity, and not a woman with emotions and desires and dreams that went beyond being a well-trained, subdued wife and hostess to a successful man who merely saw her as an asset. Just like the role her mother, Cassandra, played to Samantha's father—a beautiful and dutiful wife who enjoyed her elevated status and all the perks of being a wealthy and prominent Jamieson.

"Cassandra already bought an engagement ring she knows is Samantha's taste and style, which saves you from that tedious task," her father continued in a business-like tone. "All you have to do is put the ring on my daughter's finger, and Cassandra will start the wedding preparations."

Samantha would have no say. Not in the groom, the ring, or in her future. The assumption that she'd automatically say yes prompted her to move into the study and take control of her own life.

Without knocking, she pushed the door open the rest of the way and walked into the room, startling both men with her sudden and unexpected appearance.

She stopped next to the leather chair Harrison was

sitting in and met his wary gaze. "I'm not marrying you, Harrison, so don't bother asking."

"Samantha." Her father barked her name as a reprimand, using the harsh tone of voice that would normally bring her back in check.

Not this time. She stood her ground, refusing to give in or back down. She realized in that moment that she was facing a pivotal point—obeying her parents as she'd always done or finally living her life for herself.

Harrison's lips flattened into a thin line. "I take it you overheard our conversation?"

He didn't even have the grace to look guilty for getting caught bartering her for a promotion at Jamieson Global. "I heard every word. I'm not a piece of property for either of you to use to secure a business deal."

Neither man denied her statement, and her frustration and anger grew.

"Don't you think you're overreacting?" Harrison asked in a placating tone as he stood up, forcing her to tip her head back to look up at him.

He was lean and tall, and she hated when he used his height in a way that was meant to assert his authority over her. It was something she'd begun to notice lately, that if Harrison didn't get his way, he resorted to subtle intimidation tactics.

"I'm hardly *overreacting*." Her mother had often called her obstinate, and Samantha didn't hesitate to embrace that tenacity now. "I don't love you, and you don't love me." In the eight months of them dating, they'd never said those words to one another. Their relationship had lacked intimacy and passion and respect—all the things that made a person fall in love—and Samantha refused to spend her life in a loveless marriage, as her own mother had, for the sake of the family business.

Harrison pushed his hands into the front pockets of his slacks, impatience etching his features. "I care about you, Samantha. That's enough for me."

She shook her head, while her father stood by, saying absolutely nothing. He wouldn't change his mind and stand up for what *she* wanted. None of this was really about *her*, anyway.

"It's not enough for *me*. I want more than just you caring about me. I *deserve* better, and I will *not* marry you. Ever."

Conrad sighed in extreme annoyance. "Stop being so dramatic, Samantha. The arrangements have been made. You and Harrison *will* be getting married."

The mandate made her stomach pitch, because she knew if she stayed in this house, she'd eventually end up Harrison's wife. "It's going to be hard to have a wedding when there isn't a bride," she said, then turned and headed for the door.

"Where are you going?" her father demanded.

That booming tone never failed to make her heart race in apprehension and usually caused her to obey. But she showed no signs of fear as she stopped and faced her father again. "I don't know where I'm going, and I don't care. I'm leaving this house, and I'm not coming back anytime soon. Not until you accept that I will not marry a man I don't love."

Conrad narrowed his gaze, his expression shrewd. "If you walk out of this house tonight, you leave with nothing but the clothes on your back."

Her father wasn't bluffing. The threat was real, because Conrad Jamieson would do *anything* to ensure he won this battle of wills. He very well could win, considering she depended on her parents for everything—a deliberate tactic on their part, and now she knew why. But she was more than a pawn in her father's business, and if she hated how weak and vulnerable her dependency made her feel, it was time she did something about it. The threat of being cut off from the conveniences she'd always taken for granted was a terrifying prospect. But not as terrifying as remaining subservient to her father, marrying Harrison, and being miserable for the rest of her life.

Decision made, she continued her exit out of the study.

"Don't worry, she'll be back," she heard her father reassure Harrison. "She's not going to get very far without any financial resources."

Tears of anger tightened in Samantha's throat, and she swallowed them back. The fact that her father thought she was that incapable of taking care of herself felt like a knife in her heart and only helped to solidify her need to prove him wrong.

She rushed into the hall and nearly ran into her mother, who was standing just outside of the study, so beautiful and ageless, courtesy of fillers and plastic surgery. Judging by the horrified look on her face, she'd done her share of eavesdropping tonight, as well.

"Samantha, you can't leave," Cassandra said, a desperate note to her voice. "Why don't we have Maggie make us a cup of tea and we can talk about this."

Samantha loved Maggie—their sweet, kind, live-in housekeeper for the past twenty years. The older woman who'd rocked her to sleep at night when her own mother couldn't be bothered and who'd dried her tears when some boy hurt her feelings.

Samantha swallowed hard and held firm to the choice she'd made. "There's nothing to discuss, Mother. I love you, but I won't be bartered in a business deal, and I won't marry a man I don't love."

"Don't be ridiculous, Samantha. Let's sit down and talk. You can't possibly mean to leave all this behind."

"My life has to be about more than *this*," she said, encompassing everything around her with a wave of her hand—the ostentatious twelve-thousand-square-foot estate home they lived in and the wealth and opulence she'd grown up with that had provided her with the best of everything.

"Your father is right. You're not going to get very far before you realize what a huge mistake you've made," Cassandra said in an attempt to change her mind.

She smiled sadly at her mother. "That's a chance I'll have to take."

She headed to the foyer and grabbed the Louis Vuitton handbag she'd left on the entry table earlier and kept walking right out the massive double front doors. Car keys in hand, she slid into the Maserati GranTurismo her parents had given her on her twenty-fifth birthday. Her mind never stopped churning as she drove away from the massive estate in River Forest, until she'd reached the outskirts of Chicago.

Knowing it was just a matter of time before her father tracked her car to its location, she pulled into a parking lot of a twenty-four-hour grocery store. She brought her car to a stop in a front row slot so the security guard on duty would be able to keep an eye on the vehicle for a few hours. Because she was sure that's all it would take for her father to locate the Maserati.

She had a small amount of cash on her, and there was no telling how much longer she'd have access to her credit cards before they were put on hold. She called a cab company, then got out of the car, tossed the keys and cell phone beneath the seat—since her father could track that, as well—and manually locked the door.

Within minutes, a taxi pulled up to where Samantha was waiting. The driver was a friendly young girl in her early twenties, and she was counting on the other woman to find her just the right place to celebrate her first night of freedom. A place where no one knew her or would judge her or would expect her to be the good girl she'd always been.

"My name is Angie." The girl glanced over her shoulder to the backseat with a friendly smile. "Where can I take you tonight?"

"To your favorite bar in the Chicago area."

Angie's brows rose in surprise as she took in Samantha's designer purse and high-end attire. "Are you sure about that? My favorite bar is a far cry from The Aviary," she said of the upscale lounge where the wealthy went to mingle and be seen. "The place I hang out at is a bit on the...unrefined side," she said with a laugh.

Samantha grinned. "That's exactly what I'm counting on."

# Chapter Two

C LAY KINCAID TOOK one look at the woman sitting at the far end of the bar and immediately pegged her as a cupcake—a term one of his female bartenders had coined for a lightweight drinker who couldn't handle her liquor. Which seemed to be the case with the stunning blonde beauty who was studying the empty shot glass in front of her.

Then again, she could have been a *cupcake* for a whole other reason. She looked rich, sweet, and decadent, like the kind of irresistible gourmet treats he'd stared longingly at as a little boy from the outside of a bakery shop in town. He'd never had the chance to sample any of those sweets, but even now, at thirty-two, he could still remember the way his mouth would water for a taste, and how his always empty stomach would grumble and ache—until the shop owner chased him away because she didn't want a low-life

Kincaid, and the bastard child of a crack whore, to keep her customers from entering her upscale bakery.

This female version of a cupcake was just as tempting, and his wicked thoughts turned to taking a delicious bite out of her to see if she was as sugary as she looked, followed by licking her soft, creamy skin and defiling that perfect pink mouth and curvy body designed for pleasure and sin.

His dick twitched at the fantasy playing through his mind, but that's all it would be. A filthy fantasy. The woman clearly wasn't from the area. With that silky, shiny hair, her flawless complexion, and the strand of shimmering pearls around her neck, she screamed upper class and wealth. The rest of her attire—a pale pink silk blouse and cream-colored slacks—was also a direct contrast to the casual jean-and-T-shirt atmosphere of Kincaid's.

He moved behind the bar, where Tara, his last bartender of the evening, was mixing a drink. At ten forty-five p.m. on a Sunday night, she'd just announced last call, which was what had brought Clay out of his back office, to relieve Tara of her post by eleven. Since it was the slowest night of the week and Kincaid's was usually empty by ten after the hour, he didn't mind closing up the place by himself.

"Who's the cupcake at the end of the bar?" Clay asked Tara in a low tone of voice.

"I have no idea," Tara said with a shrug as she poured half an ounce of Kahlua into a shot glass. "I've never seen her here before."

The pretty bartender, with her long, dark hair, exotic eyes, and a diamond piercing above her upper lip, was an intriguing combination of soft and tough. Soft with a huge heart, yet tough enough to handle any man's bullshit. And considering how drunk and disorderly some of the male patrons could get sometimes, knowing that Tara was street smart and could kick ass when needed was one of the main reasons he'd hired her. The woman was fearless, as well as one helluva bartender.

Leaning a hip against the low counter, Clay let his gaze stray back to the blonde, who had her chin propped in her hand. Her entire body was relaxed, and even from the other end of the bar, he recognized the glassy, dazed look in her eyes that indicated she was well on her way to being drunk.

"Did she arrive with anyone?" he asked curiously.

Tara added an equal amount of Bailey's to the shot glass. "Nope. She came in alone."

"Is she lost?" It was the only thing that made sense to him.

"I don't think so," Tara replied, her mouth quirking with a grin as she topped the drink off with a generous amount of whip cream. "She slid onto that barstool, told me she wanted the dirtiest-named drink on the menu, so I served her a Royal Fuck. She downed the shot in one gulp and ordered two more, then told me to keep them coming, the stronger and the dirtier, the better. After three Royal Fucks, she's gone through a Screaming Orgasm, a Slow, Comfortable Screw, and a Blow Job. She's following that up with a Deep Throat," she said, lifting the sexually explicit drink she'd just made.

Clay couldn't help the amused laughter that escaped him. Damn. So, the cupcake had a bit of a naughty streak hidden beneath that affluent facade. And he had to admit, he was intrigued and wondered what had brought her to a rougher side of the city, when someone like her should have been sipping Cosmopolitans with her socialite friends in a safe, trendy lounge off of Lakeshore Drive.

Tara delivered the drink to the woman, then headed onto the main floor to clear off tables and make sure that the few customers still left didn't want a final drink before the place closed. Clay started putting bottles of alcohol away while covertly watching the blonde as she dipped her tongue into the froth of whipped cream before she wrapped her lips around the rim of the shot glass, tipped her head back, and *deep-throated* the concoction, just as the drink name implied.

*Oh, fuck me…*

A soft moan escaped her as she swallowed. When she was done, she slowly licked the remnants of whipped cream from the corner of her mouth, her lashes falling half-mast. Her actions were so guileless and unpracticed, yet so fucking sexy it turned him on—and reminded him that it had been much too long since he'd gotten laid.

One quick text to the woman with whom he had a

friends-with-benefits arrangement could easily change that status, but first he needed to make sure the cupcake left his establishment safely, then he could close up the bar. Considering his reaction to the out-of-his-league blonde, he definitely needed to indulge in a hard, hot fuck.

Tara returned with a tray of empty glasses and set them in the sink behind the bar. The last of the customers filtered out for the night, and two of his regulars gave him a wave on their way toward the exit.

"See you later, Saint," one of the older guys called out.

Clay was more a sinner than any kind of saint, but ever since his brother Mason had given him the nickname years ago to irritate him—which it had—everyone had followed suit. And the nickname stuck. It had been easier to put up with the label than fight it.

"'Night, Ted. Charlie." He lifted his hand in a reciprocal good-bye. "Be safe out there."

Tara grabbed a damp rag and started to help him with the cleanup.

"I'll finish up here," Clay said to her. "I know you have a mid-term exam tomorrow, so go home and study and get a good night's sleep before your class in the morning." Tara was attending college part-time to get her business degree, and Clay tried to support her in any way he could.

She smiled at him, her expression relieved. "Thank you. I appreciate that. I'll get the blonde to close out her tab, then head out."

"Don't worry about it." He placed a bottle of Grey Goose vodka back on the liquor shelf. "She's the last customer. I'll take care of her."

"Of course you will, *Saint* Clay," she said on a teasing drawl. "She definitely has that damsel-in-distress vibe about her, despite her expensive clothes and accessories."

Clay had a history—more like a *bad habit*—of helping and/or rescuing those who were down on their luck in some way, including Tara herself, though she'd come a long way from the broken, angry girl he'd originally employed at Kincaid's. Hell, most of his workers had been hired based on their desperate need of a paycheck, as well as a way to prove their self-worth. A lot of them came from less-than-ideal circumstances, or were trying to recover from a hellish past as damaged as Clay's own was.

But the blonde wasn't any of those things, and he doubted she needed any kind of rescuing—and certainly not from him. She was merely a pretty inconvenience, one that required Clay to do the dutiful thing, as he would with any of his customers who had had a few drinks too many.

With his back to the blonde and still facing Tara, he crossed his arms over his chest and gave her a pointed look. "I'll take care of her like I would any other tipsy patron," he said, his tone direct. "She'll pay her bill, and I'll call a cab to take her home so she's not driving under the influence. Making sure she leaves safely is all part of my responsibility as owner of this bar. Nothing more."

Tara reached up and patted his cheek. "You can try and justify it all you want, but you're a good guy, Saint Clay."

Despite his nickname and the reason behind it, he wasn't a fucking saint. Never had been and never would be. He'd done a shitload of illegal and immoral things he wasn't proud of in his life, and while he'd done his best to redeem himself, there was still a darkness inside of him that would always remain.

"Good night, Tara," he said, his abrupt tone making it clear that he was done with this conversation.

"See you tomorrow night, boss," she said with a cheeky grin.

She grabbed her purse and jacket from a cupboard behind the bar just as the dishwasher—a young kid he'd caught rummaging through the dumpster in the back for scraps to eat a few months ago—came out from the back area, where the small kitchen was. He was pushing a beaten-up bike, which was his mode of transportation that he kept in the storeroom so it didn't get stolen. A plastic bag hung from the handlebar, and Clay knew it held a Styrofoam container of leftover appetizers from happy hour. Taking a meal home at the end of the night was something Clay had insisted on, since he suspected that was the kid's main source of nutrition.

"Elijah, walk Tara to her car on your way out?" he asked the kid. Clay usually escorted his female employees to the parking lot himself at the end of the night, but for liability purposes, he wasn't about to leave the blonde completely alone for any length of time.

"Yes, sir," Elijah said respectfully, that belligerent chip on his shoulder he'd carried for the first few weeks of employment now a distant memory.

Clay waited until the two were gone and he heard Tara lock the main door before he turned around to deal with the blonde. He strolled toward her end of the bar, where she was running her finger along the rim of her shot glass, her chin propped in her hand. As he approached, her heavy-lidded gaze shifted his way, then slid down the length of his body, blatantly checking him out.

When her bluer-than-blue eyes found their way back up to his face, a soft sigh escaped her lips. "You are sooo freakin' hot," she said, her unfiltered comment a good indication that she was well and truly intoxicated. Then she glanced down at her empty glass and frowned. "I think I need another Royal Fuck, or maybe you could give me a Screaming Orgasm." She giggled like a naughty little girl, so cute and impish. "I've never asked a guy for a Screaming Orgasm before, but that last one was so good I want another."

The corner of his mouth twitched with undeniable amusement. Damn, he didn't want to like her. Didn't want to see her as anything more than the rich, privileged woman she appeared to be. The *inconvenience* he'd referred to earlier, and it was that thought that prompted him to put an end to her evening.

He took the shot glass from her fingers and set it

in the sink beneath the bar. "I think you've had enough Royal Fucks and Screaming Orgasms for tonight, Cupcake."

"Cupcake?" Her pretty eyes lit up, her complexion rosy and flushed from the alcohol. "I like cupcakes. I like to make them, and I like to eat them. And when no one's looking, I like to lick the frosting," she said in a low, secretive whisper.

Fuck. He wanted to lick *her* frosting, starting with her lush mouth and moving to her full breasts and tight nipples, then working his way lower, where she no doubt tasted sweeter than sugar. Those dirty thoughts sifted through his mind, along with a sudden jolt of arousal that had him gritting his teeth.

His physical attraction to her was unlike anything he'd ever experienced, so raw and hot and immediate. She wasn't even close to being his type of woman, but she was such an enigma, and the kind of temptation he knew would be nothing but trouble. With a shake of his head—mainly to jog some sense into his brain—he went to the register and printed up her bill. When he turned back around, he found her gaze in the vicinity of where his ass had been, and she was now shamelessly eyeing his crotch.

She slowly licked her lips and raised her glassy eyes back to his. "That Blow Job I had was pretty tasty, too," she said huskily, a faint hint of wickedness in her voice. "Maybe I'll have another one of those."

A hotter-than-fuck image of her soft, pink lips wrapped around his cock as she sucked him off emblazoned itself in his mind. His unruly dick was totally on board with that idea, and he swallowed back a groan.

Jesus Christ, she was *killing* him.

"The bar is closed and it's getting late." He placed the slip of paper on the bar in front of her. "If I can get you to settle your tab, we'll get you on your way." And he was certain he'd never see her again, thank God.

That frown came back again, along with a hint of worry creasing her brows. She reached into her purse, fumbled around the contents for a few seconds, then withdrew a wallet with the same pattern that was on her handbag. With clumsy fingers, she tried to slide a credit card from its slot, and when she finally managed the feat, she gave it to him.

He stared for a moment at the American Express Black Card. He'd heard that they existed, knew that the exclusive credit card was reserved for the obscenely wealthy, but had never seen one before. His bar clientele was strictly blue collar and paid in cash or with a standard credit or debit card. As he walked back to the register, he glanced at the name imprinted on the plastic card.

Samantha Jamieson.

Yeah, she looked like a Samantha, he thought, and ran the card through the system. A few seconds later, the word *DECLINED* showed up on the display. Certain that was a mistake, he swiped it again…and the reply remained the same.

Holy shit. Had she really maxed out one of the highest-limit credit cards available? He hadn't seen that coming. He returned to Samantha, but before he could say anything, she looked up at him with wide, knowing eyes.

"It didn't work, did it?" she asked in a pained voice.

"Umm, no," he replied, and handed her back the card. "Do you have a different one you'd like to use?" He was certain she had half a dozen credit cards to choose from.

She swallowed hard and shook her head. "No. None of them will work," she said softly, disbelief etching her beautiful features. "He really did it. My father completely cut me off," she mumbled in resignation.

Before he could process that interesting statement, she swayed on her chair, and Clay instinctively reached across the bar to grab her arms before she fell off her seat and ended up on the floor on her ass. She clutched his forearms as she tilted to the side again.

"The room is starting to spin." Her eyes squinted in a frown as she tried to focus on him. "And you look…a little fuzzy."

Oh, yeah, the cupcake was drunk. He no longer cared about her bill, but he needed to figure out what to do with *her*. "Samantha, I need your cell phone so I can call someone to pick you up."

"Got rid of it," she murmured as she pressed her fingers to her temple. "Don't want my father to find me."

Her responses were getting stranger and stranger, and he had no idea if what she was speaking was the truth or the alcohol talking. Who got rid of their cell phone because they were worried someone would find them—unless they were running from trouble? And now she was *his* problem. Fucking great.

He gently pulled her forward so her arms were resting on the counter, supporting most of her weight so she didn't tip to the side again. He quickly moved around the bar, then turned her around on the chair so that she was facing him. She blinked up at his face, looking so sad, so forlorn, that he felt an odd tightening in his chest.

He exhaled a frustrated stream of breath. "There has to be *someone* I can call. Or how about I get your address from your driver's license and have a cab take you home—"

She shook her head wildly, sending that cloud of silky blonde hair cascading over her shoulders. "I can't go home. Don't make me go back home."

He *really* wanted to be a cold, cruel bastard and send her home anyway so she was no longer his headache, but considering her emotional state, and the alcohol in her system, she was at a huge disadvantage and would never be able to deal logically with whatever she was running from.

*Fuck, fuck, fuck.*

She reached out and clutched a handful of his T-shirt, her eyes shimmering with moisture. "Oh, God, what have I done? I don't have…anything. I don't have any money, nowhere to go…" As if finally realizing how dire her situation was, she threw herself against his chest and burst into tears.

The woman had no boundaries, because she was suddenly plastered against him, her arms around his neck and her face buried against his throat as she had a mini breakdown—and he somehow became her lifeline. He was used to handling obnoxious drunks and disorderly bullies that came through the bar, but this… He had no clue what to do with a clingy, emotional female—and one that smelled so soft and deliciously feminine.

He tentatively wrapped an arm around her waist to make sure her legs didn't give out on her, all too aware of the crush of her breasts against his chest, and how her curvy body fit his in all the right places. And, yeah, his stiffening cock noticed, too, and didn't hesitate to make his interest known.

She finally calmed down and sniffled, and he almost laughed when she rubbed her runny nose against his T-shirt. The act was so unladylike, so unrefined, that he was certain she'd never do such a thing if she were clear-headed. But it made her seem more vulnerable and real. Not at all the cool, aloof socialite he'd originally pegged her for.

She let out a soft, shaky exhale, and her damp breath caressed the side of his neck. "I'm so tired, and I don't know what to do, where to go…" Her whispered words trailed off, and she snuggled closer, trusting him, *a stranger*, with her welfare.

Clay clenched his jaw and made a quick, split-second decision he prayed he didn't come to regret later. She was in no shape to go anywhere, and he wasn't such an asshole that he'd just send her on her way to fend for herself, when she was clearly high on alcohol and her judgment was skewed.

He grabbed her purse, kept an arm secured around her waist, and guided her toward the back of the bar while shutting down the lights in the place as they went. She was wobbly on her heels, and she didn't even question where he was taking her, just accepted that he was a nice guy and would keep her safe. Which was incredibly stupid on her part. He could have been a serial killer, for all she knew, and that thought just reinforced his decision to take her to his apartment upstairs and let her sleep off the liquor she'd consumed. And in the morning—and he was betting she'd be nursing a helluva hangover—she would be on her way and would no longer be his worry.

Getting her up the steps and keeping her steady on her feet was a test of his patience. She giggled each time she tripped, her mind already forgetting about the meltdown she'd just had at the bar as she flirted with him and told him once again how *freakin' hot* he was. He really wanted to be annoyed, and he would have been if she'd ended up being high maintenance, but she was actually kind of adorable...until he got her into his apartment and her face suddenly turned pale.

She pressed a hand to her stomach and licked her

dry lips, a panicked look in her eyes. "I'm so dizzy, and I don't feel so good."

*Oh, shit.* Clay knew exactly what was coming, and also knew the eruption wasn't going to be pretty considering the array of drinks she'd had. Dropping her purse on the couch, he rushed her to the one bathroom in the small apartment, which was connected to the only bedroom in the place.

She started to moan, and he curled his fingers around the back of her neck and pushed her to her knees in front of the toilet just as she started to heave. He wasn't quick enough. She started to throw up before her head was over the bowl, and a very colorful concoction splashed onto her silk blouse and expensive-looking pants before he could finally get her positioned over the commode. Even then, her hair fell around her face as she puked, and chunks of gross shit caught in the blonde strands.

Clay grimaced and swore beneath his breath as he did his best to pull her hair back while she continued to throw up. As he waited for her to empty her stomach, he thought about all the times he'd stood vigil over the toilet with Mason during his brother's wild and out-of-control teenage years. Hell, Mason was still wild and rebellious, but at least Clay was no longer responsible for sobering him up, thank God.

As the oldest with two younger brothers, Clay had been forced to step into the role of a father figure to Mason and Levi at the age of sixteen—or risk the three of them being separated by the foster care system. While his mother served her eighteen-month prison term for drug possession and prostitution, it had been Clay who'd made sure his brothers were fed, clothed, and made it to school every day (though Mason had spent most of his high school years ditching class so he could smoke weed or bang some chick, or sitting through detention for being a belligerent smartass to one of his teachers). There had been no father around to help at any point in their lives. Not when his mother had conceived each one of them with some nameless john she'd slept with to support her meth habit.

Another low groan from Samantha brought Clay's mind back to the present, which was where he preferred to remain. The past was filled with nothing but shitty, painful recollections that, for the most part, he managed to keep buried deep in that place inside him where he locked away his darkest memories.

Done retching, she finally pushed away from the toilet, trying to look composed despite how inelegantly she'd just thrown up and how wasted she still was. He released her sticky hair, grabbed a clean washcloth, dampened it with water from the sink, then gave it to her to wash her face.

She swiped the cloth across her mouth and chin, then looked down at herself, cringing in dismay as she caught sight of her soiled clothes. "That was disgusting," she murmured in embarrassment as she looked up at him from where she was still sitting on the floor. "And now…and now I'm all messy."

Truthfully, his cupcake looked like shit and smelled just as bad. "Yeah, you're a *hot* mess, all right," he said, a hint of sarcasm lacing his voice.

She perked up ever so slightly, an impish smile curving the corner of her mouth. "No...*you're* freakin' hot," she said again.

He chuckled when she totally misconstrued the phrase *hot mess* as a compliment. Clay was undoubtedly jaded when it came to women. He wasn't amused by them, and he didn't laugh with them much, either. He didn't do relationships or romance or dating. Normally, the extent of his interaction with a woman was serving one a drink at the bar or hooking up for a quick fuck. Yet this woman was already getting under his skin and intriguing him more than was wise.

Her nose wrinkled as she finally got a whiff of herself. "I...I need to take a shower," she announced, and tried to stand.

She wavered on her heels as she tried to push herself upright, and he caught her upper arm before she fell on her face. Even then, she stumbled against his chest, smearing that foul-smelling vomit all over his T-shirt and jeans.

*Fucking great,* he thought, gritting his teeth.

Even though he agreed that she smelled offensive, there was *no way* he was letting her get into a slippery tub in her condition. "How about you put one of my shirts on and lie down on the bed and take a nap?" And when she woke up in the morning, then she could deal with getting cleaned up.

She frowned at him. "But I *stink*."

"Yes, you do." There was no denying the truth.

She pushed away from him and once again staggered in those ridiculously high shoes as she attempted to unbutton her blouse. "And my hair... It's got *stuff* in it." She made a sour face. "If I don't take a shower...the awful smell is going to make me sick again."

Her brow furrowed in concentration, but her clumsy fingers couldn't figure out how to slip a button through its hole. But judging by her determined expression, Clay knew there was nothing he could say or do to make her change her mind. Not that he blamed her. The stench was making him nauseous, as well, and he had a strong stomach.

Figuring it was best to just get this done and over with so he could put her into bed and she could pass out for the night, he brushed her hands aside and quickly unfastened her blouse. Pulling the hem from her pants, he pushed the stained and silky material off her shoulders and let it fall to the floor. She reached up to unhook her sexy, pale pink lace bra that did an incredible, mouth-watering job of displaying her full, creamy breasts like an offering, and he knew if those beauties spilled free, the temptation to touch and taste would sorely test his restraint.

Hell, *everything* about Samantha was making it difficult for him to keep his hands *off* her in a sexual way, despite the fact that she'd just puked her guts out. Letting her get naked right in front of him wasn't an option, even though his straining cock argued otherwise.

"Leave it on," he said, grateful that her uncoordinated fingers couldn't manage to unclasp her bra. Did the woman have no sense of modesty? Then again, he was well aware how alcohol could loosen a person's inhibitions, and she was obviously well beyond caring about acting appropriately. No doubt she'd be mortified in the morning, but for now, she didn't care.

"But I need to—"

"*No*," he bit out, harsher than he'd intended. In the kind of authoritative voice that normally commanded a person's attention.

She dropped her hands to her sides and exhaled a petulant sigh. "You don't have to be so grumpy," she muttered, clearly not at all fazed by his sharp tone.

Yeah, he was grumpy *and* fucking horny, and it was about to get worse. As quickly as possible, he unbuttoned and unzipped her pants, and had to bend down to help her out of her shoes, then took off the last of her clothing. Her balance faltered as she stepped out of her pants, and she reached out for something to grab, which ended up being his *hair*.

He winced as her fingers tightened in the strands, and in his current position, crouched in front of her, his face level with her blush-colored lace panties, he imagined her clutching his hair for a different reason altogether. Not to steady herself but to push his mouth between her soft, smooth thighs so he could lick her with the deft slide of his tongue and get her off.

Abruptly, he stood back up and propped her ass against the vanity for support while he removed her pearls and the diamond-encrusted watch that probably cost a small fortune. He turned on the water to let it get hot while he stripped out of his T-shirt, jeans, socks, and shoes.

She watched him as he undressed, taking in the width of his chest, and followed the definition of his abs down to the waistband of his black boxer briefs that he'd left on. Licking her lips, she stared shamelessly at the thick shaft outlined by the snug cotton. Her breathing deepened, and a flush of arousal swept across her cheeks.

"You are so freakin' hot," she whispered in awe, obviously not cognizant enough to realize just how many times she'd already told him that.

His blood heated in his veins, his own unwanted desire for her making him a little crazy because he couldn't control his reaction, despite his best efforts. He briefly considered a *cold* shower but knew that wouldn't be fair to her.

"Come on, Cupcake," he said, holding out his hand for her to grab. "Let's do this."

Her pretty blue eyes widened acutely. "We're going to do it?"

He groaned, low and deep, as she once again misinterpreted his words, though she certainly didn't look opposed to *doing it* in the way she was insinuating. "You wanted a *shower*, remember? You aren't getting in there alone when you can barely stand without falling over."

Before she could argue, he grabbed her hand and helped her step into the tub. He faced her toward the spray of hot water, and as detached as possible, he helped her wash her body, then he shampooed and rinsed the crap from her hair. This wasn't something he'd ever done with or for another woman. It was all about getting in, fucking hard, and getting out. Taking care of them? Not part of the deal. Then he made the mistake of glancing at the water running rivulets over her soft skin, turning the silk of her bra and panties into a see-through vision. His entire body pulsed with lust and need. *Fuck.*

They were in the shower for less than ten minutes, but the warmth of the water loosened her muscles and turned her lethargic, so he practically had to hold her up, which didn't help his state of arousal. By the time they were finished and he'd dried her with a towel, she was swaying unsteadily where she stood, and obviously done for the night.

In his adjoining bedroom, he grabbed a clean T-shirt from his dresser and pulled it over her head and down her gorgeous, curvy body while she yawned and her eyelids drooped sleepily. Before she could put her arms through the sleeves, he reached beneath the material and removed her wet bra, then shoved her equally wet panties down her legs, all while keeping his gaze averted.

When she was decently covered, he guided her to his bed, pulled down the sheet and comforter, and helped her up. She crawled onto the mattress and flashed him her bare, delectable ass before settling onto her back. With a groan of pure torment, he pulled the covers up to her chest.

She blinked up at him drowsily. "Thank you for taking care of me," she whispered, her lashes drifting shut.

In that moment, she looked so vulnerable and alone, and Clay felt his chest tighten with a protective instinct he had no business feeling for her. He didn't want to care about Samantha or her situation. Didn't want to get involved with whatever had prompted her to ditch her cell phone and walk into a bar on the wrong side of town to get drunk.

And he *especially* didn't want to be attracted to her, but no doubt about it, he *so* fucking was.

He'd sleep out on the couch, and by morning she'd be clear-headed and full of embarrassed regret. As for him…he'd have the night to regroup and shore up the fortitude to shut down any unwanted emotions for the *cupcake* he'd never see again.

# Chapter Three

S AMANTHA'S HEAD FELT as though it was going to explode. The pressure, the pounding, the slightest movement increased the throbbing against her skull. With a soft groan, she pried her eyelids open and squinted in the too-bright room. She didn't recognize her surroundings, and panic rushed through her, kicking up her heart rate.

As she glanced around, hazy memories of last night finally filtered through her brain, giving her a semblance of relief, which didn't last long as mortification swept through her aching body. Not only had she had *way* too many drinks, she'd flirted outrageously with a gorgeous stranger, and had to admit that it'd felt damn good to be a little bad.

She groaned out loud, only to be caught up by a harsher recollection. Her father had completely and totally cut her off, just as he'd said he would. The pounding in her skull increased to epic proportions.

Unfortunately, her humiliation wasn't finished yet. Not only hadn't she been able to pay her bar bill, she'd burst into tears in front of The Gorgeous One, blabbered about her personal woes, then vomited in spectacular fashion, missing the toilet completely. Then there was the shower, where her savior had stepped in along with her, helping her clean herself up and dress again after. Her utter mortification was complete.

Careful not to jostle her head too much, she gently rolled to her back and slung her arm over her eyes to shield them from the shaft of daylight coming in through the window. She definitely needed a few more minutes to gain her bearings before she attempted to get out of bed. Which gave her too much time to think about her behavior the evening before.

Getting drunk, on any occasion, so wasn't her. She'd never been a party girl, and she knew her limits when it came to alcohol—one cocktail and no more. Last night, she'd consumed more shots of liquor than she could remember, but they'd all tasted so good, and she'd secretly loved the fact that each drink had a dirty name. At the time, indulging in a few Royal Fucks, Screaming Orgasms, and Blow Jobs had been a fun and harmless way to thumb her nose at all the rules and social norms her parents had placed on her for so long.

But her bold act of rebellion had come at a steep price, because now she had no money, no job, no car, and no place to live. She literally had *nothing*. She was twenty-six years old and ashamed to admit that everything she owned had been *given* to her in one form or another. She'd accepted each and every item without complaint, but with her lifestyle came certain expectations that, up to this point, she'd fulfilled like a good, obedient daughter.

She couldn't live that way anymore. Tucking her tail between her legs like a bad puppy and going back home wasn't an option. Samantha knew exactly who and what was waiting for her there. More enforced decorum and etiquette, and chastisement and punishment for her defiance. No, thank you. Now that she'd had a small taste of freedom, she wanted to experience more. She wanted to live life on her terms, without restrictions, and she wanted to make her own decisions and mistakes along the way.

She didn't fool herself into believing that starting over with nothing would be easy, but somehow, she'd find a way to be independent and successful, without her parents' financial support. She needed to find herself—the woman she was without the confinements and restrictions of home.

But before she could do any of those things, she needed to haul her ass out of bed and face the day. And the hot, sexy man who'd been her savior last night. She might be mortified, but she damn well knew that without him and his kindness, she had no idea where she would have woken up this morning or what might have happened to her in the state she'd gotten herself into.

With effort, she sat up on the edge of the mattress and waited a few seconds for her head to stop spinning. Her queasy stomach growled, reminding her that she was empty inside, and her mouth tasted like... Um, no, she didn't even want to think about it.

Catching sight of her pearls and wristwatch on the nightstand, she once again counted herself lucky a decent guy had come to her rescue. She checked the time, shocked to realize that it was nearly eleven a.m. She dragged a hand through her hair and winced as her fingers snagged on the tangled strands. Obviously, The Gorgeous One hadn't used conditioner when he'd scrubbed her hair in the shower, but she was grateful that she at least smelled clean—and quite masculine, considering her skin held traces of a citrusy-fragranced body wash.

Feeling the tug of a smile, she gingerly stood up. The men's shirt she was wearing fell to mid-thigh, but it was the caress of cool air on her bare sex that brought forth another memory, of being stripped out of her wet bra and panties by very large, warm, capable hands. The man had been nothing short of a gentleman the entire evening, despite the fact she'd draped herself all over him and given him every signal imaginable that she'd be up for more. He hadn't taken advantage, and for that she was grateful.

She couldn't remember ever being so flirtatious and shameless with a man, but the alcohol had loosened her inhibitions, and her strong attraction to him, aided by her newfound confidence, had bolstered her courage and encouraged her brazen behavior. Well, the night was over, and she had no choice but to face him, she thought, and made her way to the adjoining bathroom to freshen up.

Considering what she remembered happening in this room the night before, everything was now clean and orderly. She used the facilities, and when she washed her hands, she noticed a brand new tooth-brush in its original packaging sitting by the sink. Grateful for his thoughtfulness, she vigorously brushed the fuzziness from her teeth and gargled with the mouthwash on the vanity. When she finally looked in the mirror, the reflection staring back startled the hell out of her.

She looked like the hot mess he'd called her last night. Her normally straight blonde hair was wavy and disheveled—a far cry from the smooth, sleek, silky style that her mother insisted she wear. Any trace of makeup was gone, and her face was scrubbed clean except for the smudge of liner around her eyes.

She had a few makeup items in her handbag, but she had no idea where her purse was. Or her clothes, for that matter, though she did find her bra and panties hanging over the shower rod. They were dry to the touch, and she slipped on her underwear, feeling much better about greeting her white knight while wearing panties. With a deep, fortifying breath to calm the sudden flutter of nervous butterflies in her stom-ach, she opened the bedroom door, which led directly into a small living room and attached kitchen. The place was incredibly compact and sparsely furnished, and she found *him* quite easily.

Sitting at a small dining table with four chairs, he was hard to miss. Not because of his size—though he was tall and well built everywhere—but because of his commanding presence that made her very aware of him physically. He watched her from across the room, a speculative look in his gaze. His hair was a rich chocolate brown, his eyes equally dark and intense. Not to mention shrewd and perceptive.

Even from a distance, his discerning gaze made her shiver. Her skin prickled, and her entire body flushed with heat, rendering her breathless. A deep inhale of much-needed oxygen, and her breasts rose beneath the cotton T-shirt she wore. Her sensitive nipples rasped across the material, puckering them into tight, hard points that beaded against the fabric.

Even in the light of day, without the interference of any liquor, her attraction to him was instantaneous and undeniable. Thrilling and unlike anything she'd ever felt or experienced with Harrison…or any other man, for that matter. A sizzling heat settled deep in her belly, and a sudden aching need coiled between her thighs.

Oh, yeah, he was *still* freakin' hot.

Judging by the way his gaze lowered ever so slightly and the nearly negligible clench of his jaw, he'd noticed her body's response. Closing the open laptop on the table in front of him, he lifted his eyes back up to her face, his expression carefully composed.

"Morning," he murmured in a low, deep voice that was sexier than she remembered. Combined with the dark, rugged scruff on his chiseled jaw, the man was a woman's sinful fantasy come to life. He had a bit of a bad-boy edge to him that tempted the good girl in her to take a walk on the wild side.

The thought was incredibly inviting.

She tugged absently on the hem of the shirt. "Hi," she replied as she forced herself to move toward him. She smiled, suddenly feeling shy because the man had literally seen her at her worst.

"Have a seat." He gestured to the chair across the table from him.

She had no idea what to expect of him, but at least he wasn't kicking her out right away. When she was settled, he stood up and walked into the kitchen. With his back to her—God, he had a great ass in those soft, worn jeans—he filled a glass of water, then shook out a few pills from a bottle before heading back toward her.

"How are you feeling this morning?" he asked, but considering he set the water and ibuprofen on the table in front of her, he knew exactly how badly she was suffering.

"Better than last night," she admitted sheepishly. "But my pounding head and sore body are clearly protesting all those drinks I indulged in."

The faintest hint of amusement twitched the corner of his mouth. "Yeah, you're definitely a cupcake."

She recalled him using the term with her a few times. "Why do you keep calling me that?" she asked, right before she tossed all four tablets into her mouth and washed them down with most of the water, which tasted delicious sliding along her parched throat.

"Because you're a lightweight and can't handle your liquor."

She couldn't even be offended by his statement, because it was the truth.

He grabbed the mug from his end of the table and returned to the kitchen. "Want some coffee?" he asked as he refilled his own cup.

She wasn't sure that coffee would help her hangover, but hopefully the caffeine would give her a much-needed jolt of energy to figure out her next plan of action. "Sure. With cream if you have it."

He moved around the kitchen for a few minutes, and something to Samantha's left caught her attention. She glanced over and found a gray-striped cat sitting on the nearby windowsill, lazily licking its paw and cleaning its face. At first she thought one of its eyes was closed, then realized that the socket had been sealed shut and the feline was *missing* an eye.

"Here you go," he said, placing the mug down, along with a plate with dry toast on it. "You need something in your stomach."

He sounded and acted as though he'd done this a time or two, or more. "Thank you..." Her words trailed off because they'd never been formally introduced. "I don't even know your name." Though he somehow knew hers, because he'd used it last night.

"It's Clay." He leaned back in his seat and took a drink of his steaming coffee. "Clay Kincaid."

*Kincaid* matched the name of the place the cab driver had dropped her off at. "So, the bar is yours?"

"Yes."

He wasn't much of a conversationalist, but what did she expect? It wasn't as though they had some kind of relationship and he'd *invited* her to spend the night. She picked at her toast and took small bites while searching for something to fill the awkward silence between them.

"How did your cat lose its eye?" she asked curiously.

"I found her behind the bar when she was just a kitten," he said as he glanced at the feline with a fond smile. "She was scrawny as hell, full of fleas and mites and eating bugs to survive, and her left eye was badly infected. I'm not sure what caused the wound, but I took her to the vet, and they had no choice but to remove the eye and stitch it shut."

The fact that this man had rescued such a helpless creature made Samantha even more infatuated with him. "And you kept her."

"She needed a home."

He shrugged as if it were no big deal, but she knew he could have taken the cat to a shelter and not spent the money on an expensive operation to save the weak and defenseless animal. But she was quickly coming to realize that Clay Kincaid was a man who took care of people, and things—just as he'd come to her rescue last night.

"What's her name?" she asked, and took a drink of her coffee.

"Xena."

Samantha grinned. "Because she's a warrior?"

He nodded. "And a survivor."

As if the cat knew they were talking about her, she jumped down from the windowsill and scampered over to Clay's chair and meowed. Without hesitating, he reached down, scooped her up, and settled the feline on his lap. Xena rubbed up against his chest affectionately, and shamelessly head-butted his hand for him to pet her, which Clay did. Within seconds, the cat was purring contentedly.

Samantha ate the last of her toast as she watched Clay's big, strong hand stroke along Xena's spine in a slow, soft caress that made her jealous of the cat and made her wonder what it would feel like to have Clay's palm sliding over *her* body and his fingers touching her so attentively. The seductive image in her mind made her shift restlessly in her seat, and she forced her thoughts to a much safer topic. Like apologizing for her uncharacteristic behavior the evening before.

She cleared her throat, which caused him to shift his attention from Xena to Samantha's face. His dark gaze focused on her mouth longer than was polite or casual, then lifted to her eyes. There was enough heat in the depths of those brown orbs to tell her that this crazy fascination she felt toward him was mutual, even if he was better at keeping his attraction under control.

Samantha absently licked her bottom lip and spoke while she still had his attention. "Clay…I'm really sorry about last night."

He raised an eyebrow. "Which part?"

She couldn't tell if he was teasing or not, he was that good at keeping his emotions concealed. "*All* of it, but especially about getting sick, and you having to deal with me staying here at your place because I had nowhere else to go."

He continued to pet Xena, who was now curled on his lap, with her furry tail wrapped around his wrist. "Where are you going to go this morning?"

"I…I don't know," she replied honestly. She hadn't thought beyond leaving her parents' estate and escaping their rules and expectations, and she didn't feel any differently this morning. "But I'm not going back home."

A frown formed, and concern flashed in his eyes. "Samantha, are you in some kind of trouble?" His voice was low and deep and direct. "Last night you said something about your father cutting you off, and that you got rid of your cell phone because you didn't want him to find you."

She cringed. Yeah, that sounded bad. Really bad. She wasn't in a *dangerous* kind of trouble, but considering everything Clay had done for her this far, she owed him the truth. She *wanted* him to know the truth, because she desperately needed to talk to someone about her predicament. She had a few girlfriends, but none of them would understand her reasons for leaving home and turning her back on such a luxurious life, and they would criticize her for refusing to marry a successful man like Harrison even though they didn't love one another. She'd learned last night that *love* didn't factor into business mergers.

The life Samantha had walked away from was so superficial and one-dimensional, and it wasn't a world in which she wanted to live in any longer. It was a scary thought, being alone and on her own, in a rougher part of the city, without any money or a place to live, but there was no doubt in her mind that the alternative—heading home and accepting Harrison's proposal—would eventually destroy her.

Which meant she needed Clay's help.

PATIENCE WASN'T ONE of Clay's strongest traits, but persistence was. Right now, he was straddling the line between the two as he waited for Samantha to answer the question he'd asked about her being in some kind of trouble, because that was his main concern. If she was facing some kind of threat, he'd make sure she had help and support. His brother Levi was a cop, and sometimes having a sibling in law enforcement came in handy. Though Mason, the delinquent in the family who'd spent most of his youth *breaking* the law, would beg to differ.

From across the table, he continued to watch Sa-

CARLY PHILLIPS & ERIKA WILDE

mantha struggle with some kind of internal battle, and quietly let her sort things out in her head. She'd trusted him with her welfare and care last night, although, in truth, she'd been too drunk to do much of anything except let him have his way. He clenched his jaw at the thought of what could have happened to her if anyone but him had found her in such an inebriated, defenseless state. Still, he hoped she'd come to the conclusion that she could trust him now, so he could make sure she remained safe.

After a few more moments, she exhaled a deep breath, met his gaze, and spoke. "I'm not running from trouble, and I'm not in any danger. But it's true that I don't want my father to find me."

It was a start, at least. "Why not?"

"Have you ever heard of Jamieson Global?" she asked quietly.

He nodded. Jamieson Global was a huge conglomerate and one of the biggest, most well-known investment firms in Chicago. He didn't know the business on a personal level, but the name was familiar enough to most people who lived in or near the city.

In the next second, realization dawned as he made the connection...Samantha *Jamieson*.

Fuck. He stared at her in shock, feeling as though someone had just punked him. Even Xena, sensing the sudden tension stiffening his body, jumped off his lap.

The moment he'd seen Samantha in the bar, he'd suspected that she came from an affluent family, but *holy shit*, this propelled her into another stratosphere of wealth. The kind that was untouchable and way out his realm and the modest life he lived. A woman like her had absolutely no business being on *his* side of town.

"Yes, *that* Jamieson," she confirmed, taking advantage of his stunned silence. "I found out last night that my father expects me to marry the man I've been dating for the past eight months. His name is Harrison Blackwell III, and my father has been grooming him for the CEO position, which apparently comes with the stipulation that Harrison marries me so the company stays in the family."

Her blue eyes blazed with indignant anger, though Clay wasn't sure what, exactly, the issue was, considering she'd been seeing the guy for a good length of time. It wasn't as though the dude was a stranger. "Are you upset that he'll be marrying you for the promotion and to keep your father's company in the family?" he guessed.

She sat up straighter, her pretty pink lips pursed in exasperation. "No, I'm furious that my father is demanding I marry a man I don't love!"

"Demanding?" The notion seemed so archaic to him, and he couldn't tell if she was being dramatic or not.

"Yes, *demanding*. As in, not giving me a choice in the matter and expecting me to fall in line with his wishes and do as I'm told," she said, her chin jutting out stubbornly. "Being the daughter of Conrad Jamieson comes with certain obligations, and one of them is obviously an arranged marriage I have no desire to be a part of."

Her chest heaved with frustration, and Clay couldn't say that he minded the slight trembling of her unbound breasts beneath the T-shirt. She had great tits, generous and full enough to squeeze in his hands or cushion his thick cock as he tunneled his shaft between that soft flesh. Yeah, he'd spent the better part of last night tossing and turning on his couch, fantasizing about all the dirty, filthy ways he'd like to fuck her. The way her nipples would taste in his mouth, the feel of her long, gorgeous legs clutching around his hips as she came on a soft, sweet moan…

"I won't let anyone dictate who I spend the rest of my life with," she said, clearing those distracting thoughts from Clay's mind. "Especially not my father."

He forced his gaze to remain on her face. "So, you ran away from home?" he said, his tone light and teasing.

"Yes," she said, suddenly looking defeated. "I'm twenty-six years old, and that sounds so…juvenile. And yet it's one hundred percent accurate." Sighing, she combed her fingers through her wavy hair and winced as they caught on the still-tangled strands. "I'm embarrassed to admit that I've relied on my parents for everything." She didn't meet his gaze. "Honestly, I should have left a long time ago, and I hate that I've let them run my life for this long."

His coffee had gone cold, and he absently traced a finger around the rim of his cup. "So, now that you've left home, what do you intend to do?"

"I didn't have a plan beyond getting away," she admitted, then worried her teeth along her lower lip as her serious gaze met and held his. "I still don't. And I know this is more than I have a right to ask...but can I stay here until I can figure things out?" she asked quickly, the words tumbling from her lush lips. "I won't be in your way. I can sleep on the couch, and I swear you won't even know I'm around."

*Oh, fuck no.* This woman was already wreaking havoc on his self-control. He couldn't imagine her crashing in this tiny apartment, filling it with her scent, using his shower, tempting him with her mere presence.

But before he could nix her idea, she quickly continued on.

"My father *did* cut me off. Completely. I have no money, no place to stay, and I can't even pay for a hotel room or a meal." She winced in embarrassment, and her hands fidgeted in her lap before she set them back on the table. "Obviously, I didn't think things through last night, but I don't regret leaving home, and I'm determined to make it on my own. I can work at your bar to make some money until I save enough to find a place of my own, which shouldn't take long. Please?" She raised those big eyes to him.

*Was she fucking kidding?* No, the look in her wide blue eyes was completely serious and so damned determined. A part of him admired that fortitude of hers, but one look at her perfectly manicured fingernails and the soft skin on her pampered hands, and he knew she was the last person he'd ever hire to work in his bar. Within a few hours, her hands would be chapped and dry, her nails chipped, and her uncalloused feet would be screaming for relief.

She'd be an entertaining novelty to all his regular customers, and with all that wavy blonde hair, those big, guileless blue eyes, and her killer curves, she'd pose a major distraction to every man who entered the bar. As the new girl, she'd be the focus of rude comments and bold, assertive hands that wouldn't hesitate to test her limits.

The younger crowd at Kincaid's was rowdy, mouthy, and after a few drinks too many, they were assholes who didn't give a shit that Clay had a hands-off policy when it came to the women who worked for him. Tara and his other bar waitresses could handle the more aggressive advances. But Samantha? She'd be like fresh, tasty meat to a tank full of hungry sharks. She'd never survive.

She really needed to go home. "Samantha, I don't think—"

"Clay, *please*," she interrupted him before he could say no, her voice as soft and pleading as the look in her eyes. "I just need someone to give me the chance to prove myself."

And she was asking for that someone to be him.

He scrubbed a hand down his face and along his taut jaw. Her words were an echo from Clay's own past, hitting him where he was the most emotionally susceptible. *Please, Jerry, just give me the chance to show you what a hard worker I am,* a teenaged Clay had begged. *I swear, you won't be sorry.*

Jerry had given him that chance, had believed in him—the bastard child of a known crack whore—when no one else would. And that one kind gesture had completely changed Clay's, and his brothers', lives.

He didn't believe a job in his bar would alter Samantha's life in quite the same way, but he understood how difficult it was to ask someone for help when you were at your lowest. And for Samantha, this was rock bottom.

His gut told him he was about to make a monumental mistake in aiding this woman, but considering how resolute she was, he didn't doubt that if he made her leave, she'd try and find some kind of work elsewhere, and there was no telling who would try and take advantage of her. And where would she live with no money or credit cards that worked? No phone or vehicle? Who would make sure that she stayed safe in this rough area of town?

*Fuck.* His Goddamn conscience wouldn't allow him to turn her away and leave her to her own devices. A woman like her, who'd grown up in the lap of luxury, hadn't spent her youth honing her survival instincts like he and his two younger brothers had. She was too vulnerable, too defenseless, and too trusting. And there were too many people out in the world who wouldn't think twice about exploiting her naiveté.

He was going to let her live in his apartment and

CARLY PHILLIPS & ERIKA WILDE

work in the bar for the sole reason of being able to keep an eye on her so she stayed safe. There was no doubt in his mind that Samantha wouldn't last long in this environment. Maybe a few days before she realized that this kind of life was tough and unglamorous, that working for a living was hard, strenuous, and exhausting, and marrying a wealthy CEO in her own social circle—*love or no love*—was exactly what she wanted, after all. In this case, she'd quickly discover that the grass was *not* greener on the other side of the city, and she'd be happy to return to her rich life.

"Okay," he said evenly as he leaned back in his seat and crossed his arms over his chest. "Consider yourself hired as a bar waitress. You start tonight. And you can stay here until you save enough to get your own place."

He took in the T-shirt she wore, reminding him that her soiled silk top and pants were still on his washing machine because they'd had a *dry clean only* tag inside each garment. She needed practical clothes, and jeans and comfortable shoes to work in since she'd be on her feet for hours.

"I'll call my brother's best friend, Katrina, who can take you shopping for some clothes and toiletries."

The gratitude shining in her eyes was unmistakable. "I'll pay you back. For everything."

He wasn't worried about being reimbursed. He had more money than he'd ever spend in his lifetime, thanks to Jerry. His only concern was putting Samantha to work, because the sooner she experienced hard labor, the sooner she'd be on her way back home and his life could get back to normal. Which would also put an end to the fascination she presented.

Figuring they were done, he stood up, grabbed his coffee mug, and walked into the kitchen. He heard her following behind him, her bare feet padding on the hardwood floor. She set her plate and cup in the sink, then turned to face him. She took a deliberate step closer, her tongue nervously dampening her bottom lip, and the attraction and sexual tension he'd managed to keep at bay all morning flared inside of him.

The appreciation in her gaze was now gone, replaced by a feminine curiosity, and something a whole lot more tempting. Daring, even. He stood still, unsure what she intended, but he didn't have to wait long to find out. She splayed her hands on his chest, and even through the soft cotton of his shirt, her touch felt warm and far more confident than it should have.

Anticipation and heat saturated his senses, making rational thinking nearly impossible as his body responded to her slow, subtle seduction. A dangerous ache coiled between his legs, and if she shifted any closer, she was going to get acquainted with the stiffening length of his cock.

Her eyes held his as she stood up on her bare tip-toes, and with her lips less than an inch away from his, she whispered, "Thank you, Clay," right before she brushed her mouth across his and kissed him.

# Chapter Four

C LAY CURLED HIS hands into fists at his sides. He
didn't trust himself to move as Samantha gradually increased the pressure of her mouth against his, her
gratitude shifting into something more sensual and
intimate. The kiss was warm, soft, and undeniably
persistent, and a needy sigh escaped her as her tongue
flicked experimentally against his upper lip. Teasing
him. Tormenting him. And testing his restraint in a
way that was foolish and dangerous for a man like
him.

A man who didn't do soft or slow or sweet when it
came to women.

Seemingly oblivious to the sudden tension thrum-
ming through him, she slid her hands up his chest and
around his neck, bringing her body flush to his. The
heat of her firm breasts and tight nipples penetrated
through her shirt and his, making him ache for her.

The need inside him expanded, gnawing at his self-control. She had no fucking clue how close he was to feeding the hunger that had been twisting in his gut since last night.

He placed his hands on her waist, intending to push her away and end this madness so he could set some boundaries, until the vixen nipped at his lower lip and playfully tugged it between her teeth. *Oh, fuck me...*

The last bit of his self-discipline snapped, unleashing the beast inside of him. Selfish bastard that he was, Clay wasn't going to refuse sampling the pleasure she was offering. Last night, her flirtatious advances had been under the influence of alcohol. This morning, she was stone-cold sober and knew exactly what she was doing. And since this was his one and only chance to taste her, he wasn't about to hold back. She was about to experience Clay's more dominant, aggressive side, and he was certain that would be enough to shock some sense into her and show Samantha that her kind of sophistication was no match for his rough, coarse, sexual appetite.

Lifting his hands, he buried them in her hair until his fingers twisted tight around the strands to hold her to his will, and pulled her head back. She let out a startled gasp as her gaze met his, not with the wariness or panic he'd been anticipating but with a flash of excitement that made his blood sizzle in his veins. She was such a fucking contradiction, so naive and trusting in some respects, yet so daring and fearless when it came to dealing with him. The combination was lust inducing.

Before he could talk himself out of it, he crushed his mouth to hers. The kiss was hot, hard, and demanding from the moment his lips touched hers, and his tongue swept deep inside to plunder and devour. She moaned and wrapped her hands around his biceps, as if she needed something to hold on to as he continued to keep her mouth positioned beneath his and feasted on her rich, decadent flavor.

She tasted like the cupcake he'd called her. So delicious he wanted to eat her up. So sweet he couldn't get enough, no matter how much he immersed himself in the kiss. He burned for her. She trembled for him. His cock pulsed with excruciating need beneath the fly of his jeans, and lust, thick and heavy, fogged his brain.

With his mouth fused to hers, he guided her backward, until her ass hit the edge of the table they'd just been sitting at. His hands dropped to her hips, and with a slight lift, she was sitting on the flat surface. Breathing hard against her parted lips, he pushed her legs wide apart and moved in between, so that the rigid length of his erection aligned with the front panel of her panties. Even through the denim, he could feel her heat and dampness, and it drove him wild.

He thrust his tongue deep inside her mouth, matching the grind of his cock against her sex. She whimpered and shamelessly tightened her thighs around his waist. Her soft hands found their way beneath his T-shirt and skimmed over his abs and continued up to his chest, until her fingers reached his nipples and plucked at the tight, sensitive tips.

He groaned and shuddered. His dick throbbed almost painfully, and he barely managed to clench his jaw against the onslaught of relentless heat surging through him.

*What the hell was he doing?* If she'd been any other woman, he would have been balls deep inside her by now, driving them both toward a mind-bending orgasm. But he intuitively knew that Samantha Jamieson wasn't someone he could fuck mindlessly and casually walk away from afterward. She was well-bred, refined, and probably didn't venture beyond traditional missionary sex. He was rough around the edges and liked his encounters hot and sweaty and down and dirty.

He jerked back so that there were a few inches of space between them and more than enough room to put an end to their very near miss. She looked up at him, her lips wet and swollen from his kiss, her face flushed with desire, and her gaze exhilarated and oh-so-hopeful for much, much more.

It wasn't going to happen. "You're playing with the hottest kind of fire there is, Cupcake," he said, his voice tinged with an unmistakable warning.

Her chin lifted ever so slightly, and the corner of her mouth curved upward in a brazen smile. "You didn't seem to mind a few moments ago."

Jesus fucking Christ. He wanted to do dirty things to that sassy mouth of hers, wanted to *show her* how he handled impudent women in the bedroom. Resisting the urge took effort—because just imagining the feel of her bare ass quivering beneath the smack of his hand made him harder than stone—but he managed to keep his head focused on drawing those all-too-important lines between them. He needed to set her straight, establish clear boundaries between them, and the only way he knew to do that was to be blunt and crude enough to shock some sense back into her upper-class sensibilities.

Bracing his hands on the table on either side of her hips, he leaned in close and gave her his best intimidating scowl. "I'm not a gentleman, Samantha," he said harshly. "I don't do soft and gentle and sweet. I like to control and fuck so hard and deep you'll scream and be sore the next day. I'd want you on your knees, with my hands fisted in your hair while you suck my cock, and then I'd bend you over this table, spread your legs wide, and fuck you all over again."

That definitely got her attention, but not in the way he'd hoped. Her eyes widened, and her breathing deepened, and she licked her lips in a way that told him she was playing every one of those wicked scenarios through her mind.

"What...what if that's what I want?" she asked softly.

The muscles in his stomach tightened, and he exhaled a slow, deep breath as he straightened once again. "It's not going to happen." He had to be smart enough for them both. "If you're going to be staying here, we need to set some rules."

She frowned at him, jerking back in a way that told him he'd hit a nerve. "I'm twenty-six years old, and I've spent my entire life being told what to do. I'm done with rules, Clay. I'm done being a straight-laced good girl when the woman inside of me wants excitement and passion and a man who can show me both."

"I'm not that man, Samantha," he said gruffly. "You're just being wild and rebellious now that you have a little freedom, and you like the way it feels. There's no way I'm going let you do something you'd regret later."

She pursed her lips but didn't argue further, and that, more than anything, made him nervous. Whoever she'd been before, this incarnation of Samantha Jamieson clearly had no problem going after what she wanted.

And she'd made it clear she wanted him.

SAMANTHA LIKED KATRINA immediately. She was friendly, kind, and arrived at Clay's place with a tank dress and a pair of flip-flops for Samantha to wear since her blouse and pants were still dirty. Katrina was shorter and more petite in size, but the dress was cut in a way that hung loose on Samantha's body and would work until she could get something else that fit properly.

"Ready to go?" Katrina asked once Samantha

walked out of Clay's bedroom, now wearing the more comfortable outfit.

"Yes. Thank you again for the loan on the dress and shoes," Samantha said, feeling momentarily self-conscious because she'd *had* to borrow someone else's clothes. That was another first for her. "I really appreciate it."

"It's not a problem," the other woman said with a wave of her hand, though her pretty green eyes brimmed with undeniable interest. "Though I have to say, I've never known Clay to let a woman spend the night here, let alone have one move in so quickly."

Samantha felt a warm blush sweep across her cheeks, even though the smile Katrina gave her was light and teasing. She had no idea what, exactly, Clay had told the other woman about their arrangement or how she'd ended up in his apartment in the first place. As soon as he'd informed Samantha that he wasn't about to let her do something she'd regret after that hot, scorching kiss they'd shared, he'd pushed her away, muttered something about calling Katrina from his office downstairs at the bar, then he'd stalked out of the small apartment.

He'd left her sitting on the table, all alone with too many thoughts running through her head. Mainly, about how she'd never, *ever* experienced such raw passion before. And the things he'd said to her after-ward, about not being soft and gentle and sweet, well, even now her stomach clenched tight thinking about all those wicked things Clay had said he wanted to do to her. He'd meant to scare her off, but instead, he'd ignited a desire inside of her that she wanted *him* to satisfy. No other man would do after the hot, lustful way he'd claimed her mouth and made her body burn with need.

"My staying here is temporary," Samantha replied to Katrina's comment as she picked up her purse from the couch. "Until I can make some money and figure out a few things." Which she hoped would only take a few weeks, tops.

Katrina's gaze traveled from the designer bag in Samantha's hand up to her face. There was no judgment in her eyes, just curiosity, so Samantha was hopeful that the other woman thought the handbag was a knock-off. She didn't want her old life interfering with her new one, which meant the Louis Vuitton had to go, because the last thing she wanted was to draw attention to herself.

Samantha followed the other woman out a different side door and down a flight of wooden stairs to a small parking area. From what she could remember of last night, the other door in the apartment led directly to the bar downstairs, so Clay lived conveniently above the bar.

Katrina pressed the remote in her hand, and an alarm disengaged on a cute Volkswagen Beetle in a bright iridescent purple as funky as its owner, and which matched the plum-hued highlights tinting the edges of Katrina's blonde, wavy hair, as well as the shimmering polish on her nails.

Katrina was pretty, but there was a tough edge about her, from the way she walked to her overall appearance—a *don't mess with me* vibe that Samantha both admired and respected. The other woman wore tight black jeans, leather lace-up boots with a spiked heel, and a black tank top that showcased the colorful sleeve of tattoos covering her left arm and traveling up the side of her neck. The ink looked like dozens of exotic butterflies taking flight along her skin. It was a beautiful piece of art and unlike anything Samantha had ever seen on a woman before.

Then again, the ladies and friends in her social circle didn't mar their perfect skin with permanent ink. Her own mother, upon seeing a girl with a few tattoos at the grocery store, had whispered to Samantha that only heathens and trashy people got tattoos, that they were disgusting and degrading. Samantha had always felt differently, had even secretly wanted a tattoo of her own, but hadn't dared to follow through on the urge because she knew the consequences from her parents would have been severe.

That was the old Samantha, the classic good girl who always worried about disappointing her mother and father. A smile tugged at the corners of her mouth when she thought about all the rules she'd already broken in less than a day, and just how good it felt to be bad for a change. Especially when it came to Clay.

Once they were both settled into the small and surprisingly comfy car, Katrina glanced at Samantha as she turned the key in the ignition. "Clay said you'll be working as a bar waitress at Kincaid's, so you'll need some jeans and comfortable shoes, right?"

Samantha nodded, trying to read Katrina's tone, but the woman was really good at keeping her true thoughts concealed. So, she tried to explain. "I know this whole situation, with me staying with Clay and working at the bar, must look odd to you—"

"Oh, it's not odd at all," Katrina interrupted before she could finish, a small smile on her lips as she shrugged. "It's what Saint Clay does. He takes care of people."

Samantha frowned. Saint Clay? She tried to make sense of the nickname and wondered how it related to the gruff man she'd met, but before she could question Katrina, the other woman spoke.

"We'd better get moving." She put the car in reverse to back it out of the parking spot. "I have two hours before Mason expects me back at the shop, though honestly, he can kiss my ass for making *that* demand, considering I am the manager of the place and not his personal slave."

Samantha couldn't stop the grin that appeared as the other woman pulled into traffic. Oh, yeah, she liked Katrina. A lot. The girl obviously had no qualms about saying it like it was or refusing to take crap from anyone.

"Mason is Clay's brother, right?" Samantha asked.

"He's *one* of Clay's brothers, yes," Katrina said as she slipped a pair of sunglasses on her face. "There's also Levi, who's the youngest of the three."

Being an only child, Samantha had always wanted a sibling, but right after she'd been born, there had been complications that had forced her mother to have an emergency hysterectomy—which was something Samantha's father hadn't been happy about, since he'd gotten a daughter instead of the son he wanted.

"I take it they're all close?"

"You wouldn't think so when you see them interact, but to be fair, Mason can be an asshole, and he likes to push both of his brothers' buttons." Humor infused Katrina's voice before her expression turned more serious. "But yeah, they're close. The three of them have been through a lot of shit together, and there's nothing they wouldn't do for each other. That said, they couldn't be more different in looks *or* personality."

Samantha was intrigued. "In what way?"

"Well, they might not *look* like brothers, but they are all fine, hot-looking, gorgeous pieces of man candy." Katrina grinned, clearly appreciating that particular quality about the Kincaid brothers. "Personality-wise, Clay is the responsible, uptight one. Mason is and always has been the cocky hell-raiser, and Levi is the good, respectable cop who wouldn't dare color outside the lines, if you know what I mean. He's so straight-laced he squeaks."

Samantha laughed, though she had a feeling that she'd relate well to Levi considering his character, even if she was highly attracted to Clay. Mason, she wasn't so sure about. He sounded like a bad boy who enjoyed corrupting good girls, like the kind of guy her mother had warned her to stay away from as a teenager. And she'd dutifully kept her distance from those kinds of boys, even if they had fascinated her from afar.

After this morning with Clay, Samantha understood the appeal of being corrupted by a man who was bad and tough and pure alpha male. Clay's more dominant tendencies had excited her in ways she'd never known were possible, probably because the men she'd dated up to this point had been too polite, proper, and uninspiring in the bedroom.

And in Harrison's case, he liked everything clean and orderly, including any physical contact—whether that was shaking someone's hand or what the two of them did in the bedroom. His OCD affliction, combined with being a severe germaphobe, had made sex a quick and to-the-point process. There hadn't been any leisurely foreplay with mouths and fingers sliding in hot, wet places. No deep, steamy, tongue-tangling kisses that made her melt. And as soon as it was over, he'd moved off the bed to take a shower. Without her.

She'd already had plenty of *gentlemen*, along with *soft and gentle and sweet*, and that was the last thing she desired from an assertive man like Clay. She wanted to be claimed and possessed in the exact way he'd described this morning. She wanted to experience what it was like to be at the sensual mercy of Clay's hands and mouth. She wanted to feel what it was like to be pinned beneath his strong, hard body as he fucked her, giving her no choice but to accept whatever pleasure he gave her.

Samantha swallowed back a soft moan at the fantasy playing in her mind. With extreme effort, she forced herself to focus on what Katrina was saying as she continued to talk about the Kincaid brothers in an animated voice that indicated she knew all of them pretty well and was fond of each one.

"I take it you've known them a long time?" Samantha asked when Katrina stopped talking.

"I met Mason when I was fourteen and we…" She paused for a moment, as if catching herself before she said something she hadn't meant to share before continuing more tentatively. "We went to the same high school. We bonded over something we had in common, and we've been best friends since."

Samantha instinctively knew there was more to that story, but didn't want to pry. "And now you work with him?"

"Actually, I work *for* Mason," Katrina clarified as she turned the car into a large shopping center with an array of stores, with Target as the anchor. "He owns a tattoo shop a few streets over from Clay's bar that's called Inked. Mostly I manage the place and do his accounting and keep his shit together, but I also occasionally draw art for clients, though I don't do the actual tattooing."

Samantha's gaze once again took in the stunning images displayed on her skin that looked so lifelike. "Did Mason do all those butterflies on your arm and neck?"

"No. Someone else did," Katrina replied as she turned the Beetle into a parking spot.

Considering Katrina had just said that Mason was her best friend, along with the fact that she worked in his shop, Samantha was surprised another artist had tattooed her instead. "Well, they're beautiful."

"Thank you." The other woman took off her sunglasses, giving Samantha a brief glimpse of something more emotional in regard to those butterflies, before it was chased away by a light and fun smile. "Come on. Let's go get the things you need and spend some of Clay's money."

Katrina made it sound as though he had a ton of cash to burn, which couldn't be the case considering where his bar was located and the tiny apartment he lived in. Regardless, Samantha hated the thought of having to spend *any* of Clay's money. "I just need the basics to get me through to my first paycheck." And then she'd be reimbursing him for everything she bought today.

As she got out of the car and followed Katrina toward the huge retail store, the other woman glanced her way with a devious grin. "Trust me, you'll have money *before* your first paycheck. We'll get you a pair of tight-fitting jeans to wear while you're working, along with a snug Kincaid's T-shirt, and I can guarantee that the men who come into the bar will be *throwing* tips your way."

"Or *not*, since I have no idea what I'm doing," she joked, but it was the truth. Samantha would like to think that taking orders and delivering drinks would be a fairly easy thing to do, but like any job, she was sure there would be some kind of learning curve involved, and she'd make a few mistakes along the way.

Samantha could only hope that Clay didn't fire her on her first night.

# Chapter Five

CLAY MANAGED TO avoid Samantha for most of the day. While she was out with Katrina, and even after she'd returned, he'd stayed down at the bar going through liquor inventory and keeping himself busy prepping for the evening crowd. Happy hour started at four, and Monday was ladies' night, which meant half-price drinks for the women who came into the place.

The weekly promotion was great for business, but having an influx of female patrons also attracted a whole lot of men who were looking to score, and that made for a very busy night. At three-thirty, employees started to arrive—Hank, the cook, who prepped the appetizers, Elijah, who made sure all the drink glasses were cleaned and stocked for the rush of orders, along with Tara and Gina, who tended the bar, and Amanda and Tessa, who were experienced cocktail waitresses.

While Samantha had been gone earlier with Katrina, Clay had left a Kincaid bar shirt for her on the table to wear, along with a note telling her to be downstairs and ready to work at the designated time. He glanced toward the door that led up to his apartment just as it opened and the woman who'd spent way too much time in his head today appeared and walked toward the bar, where he'd just delivered a case of beer.

Damn, she looked good. He'd been worried about her fitting in with the rest of his employees, but all his concern evaporated as he watched her approach. Gone was the sophisticated, obviously wealthy-looking lady who'd come into his bar last night with the sole purpose of getting drunk. With her hair down in loose, natural waves and minimal makeup, this woman looked young and fresh and bright-eyed and eager. She looked as though she *belonged* in this environment.

He knew her attire was the main reason, and Jesus Christ, could the jeans she'd bought today be any tighter? The dark-wash denim molded to her curves, accentuating the sway of her hips, her sleek thighs, and long, slender legs. The material of the T-shirt he'd left for her to wear stretched taut across her chest, and he was a fucking idiot for feeling possessive about the way his last name, *Kincaid's*, was imprinted across her full breasts, as if it were a statement that she belonged to him, rather than the name of the bar. All he needed to add was *property of* above Kincaid's to complete the stupid-ass need to put a claim on her before any other men arrived and hit on her.

And he knew they would. Tonight's male clientele for ladies' night tended to be the cockier, more presumptuous type of guys, who, after a few drinks, became overly aggressive, rude, and lost any filter that they might have had when they'd first come in. For the most part, Clay managed to keep things under control, but he knew that Samantha was going to experience one hell of a culture shock tonight. If he was lucky, she'd be gone before the end of the night and heading back to where she'd come from.

Because he really, *really* needed her to leave. She was too much of a distraction and temptation, and proved as much when she met his gaze from across the room and gave him a sweet, sultry smile that made his cock twitch in his jeans and a groan roll up in his throat. He swallowed it back before the sound could escape.

"What the hell is she still doing here?" Tara asked from beside him, a frown on her face as her gaze traveled in the same direction as his. "And why is she wearing a bar uniform?"

"Because she needed a job," he muttered, and made himself busy shoving beer bottles into the vat of ice so he didn't have to make eye contact with Tara.

Knowing there was no way he could keep Samantha's living arrangements a secret for long, he decided to get it out in the open and be done with it.

He straightened and finally met Tara's gaze. "And since everyone is going to find out soon enough, she's staying in my apartment upstairs for a week or so."

"You've got to be joking," Tara said, her eyes widening incredulously. "I thought you said you'd take care of her like any other tipsy patron. Make sure she leaves safely and all that." She shook her head, and a tiny hint of a smile tugged at the corner of her mouth. "You just couldn't resist rescuing that damsel in distress, could you?"

He wasn't about to answer her question, and he didn't need to justify his reasons for letting Samantha stay. "Don't worry. She won't be here long."

Tara cut him a sidelong glance filled with curiosity as she set a stack of napkins on the bar top, then started refilling the swizzle sticks. "Why is that?"

"Because she's never worked at a bar, and she doesn't have a damn clue what she's in for tonight."

Tara didn't bother to hide a smirk. "So, you're hoping tonight's rowdy crowd will scare her off and send her back to wherever she came from?"

"That's the plan," he admitted. Because after this morning's encounter, he had no idea how long he could keep his hands off her. Especially when she'd already allowed him to kiss her with such lust and heat and had made it known she wanted a whole lot more of everything he had to offer. And fuck, did he want to give it to her. Badly.

Samantha finally reached the other side of the bar and sent him a cheerful smile. "I'm ready to get started. Where do you need me?" she asked, her innocent words not so innocent in Clay's dirty mind.

*On your knees in front of me...lying flat on your back with your legs wrapped tight around my waist as I slide hard and deep—*

"Since Clay seems incapable of speaking at the moment, I'm Tara," his bartender said in a wry tone, introducing herself as she waved one of the other bar waitresses over. "Let's have Amanda give you a crash course on taking drink orders and what to expect tonight."

Samantha didn't even look a little bit nervous about her first night on the job. "That would be great."

"She can help you out for the first few hours after we open," Tara went on as she placed a small rubber mat on the service bar counter. "But at some point we'll be slammed and you'll have a section all to yourself and you'll be on your own."

"It's a good thing I'm a quick learner." A too-confident Samantha turned to Amanda and introduced herself, then the two of them walked away so Amanda could give her a quick lesson on drink terminology and how their order system worked.

"Is there something going on between the two of you?" Tara asked, the amusement in her voice evident as she began slicing lime wedges. "Because for a minute there, you know, while you were staring at her like a deaf-mute, you looked like you wanted to vault yourself over the bar, tackle the woman, and do all sorts of dirty things with her." She waggled her eyebrows at him, enjoying herself immensely.

*Get the fuck out of my head, Tara.* "You have quite the

imagination." He gave her a bland look.

"Deny it all you want, Saint Clay," she said, narrowing her gaze as she pointed the knife at him to emphasize her point. "But I've never seen you look at another woman that way. Not even Vicky."

Vicky, the woman he occasionally hooked up with and who had been his casual fuck buddy for the past year. No, he'd never, ever felt this insane kind of hunger and need for Vicky as he did for Samantha, which was why she made the perfect hookup. But he wouldn't admit his weakness for Samantha to Tara, or anyone else, for that matter.

"I thought your degree was going to be in business, *not* psychoanalysis," he said in a droll tone meant to deflect her scrutiny.

The slight furrow of concern between her brows remained. "Just…be careful, Clay."

*I don't want you to get hurt.* He could see the unspoken words in her eyes, and the fact that Tara even thought that was a possibility aggravated him. There was only one woman he'd ever let get close enough to hurt him—his own mother—and the brutal devastation and anger he'd experienced after her heartless actions pretty much ensured that Clay would never give any other female that much power over him ever again.

So, no, Tara had no reason to worry about him doing something as careless and stupid as falling for Samantha, a woman he could pretty much guarantee would be gone in a few days. A week, tops. He'd bet his bar on it.

"*Nothing* is going on," he said in a voice that sounded much steadier than he felt. "I'm just helping her through a tough time in her life. That's it."

Tara opened her mouth to respond, but before anything else could spill out, Clay held up a hand and cut her off. "This conversation is over. I'm going to see if Hank needs help in the kitchen before happy hour starts."

Tara's lips pursed, but when he turned around and walked away, he heard her mutter distinctly behind him, "Stubborn ass."

Yeah, whatever. He'd been called much worse.

He went to the small kitchen in the back, where Hank was pulling huge trays of chicken wings from the oven, which he would then throw into the fryer as they were ordered. Elijah, who currently had no dishes to wash, was helping Hank prep the other items—beef sliders, chicken fingers, potato skins, and a few other appetizers.

"Everything good in here?" Clay asked.

Hank gave him his typical, jovial one-sided smile and a thumbs-up as she moved about the kitchen. "Yep, we're good, boss."

Clay watched the duo for a few more minutes, glad that he'd taken a chance on them both. They were good, hard workers, but then again, they'd not only needed a job, they'd really *wanted* the employment. For money, yes, but also to restore their dignity.

Especially Hank. He'd hired the other man a few

years ago when he'd come into Kincaid's looking for a job. *Any job.* At twenty-eight, he'd been a year out of the military and disabled, having lost one of his legs in an IED explosion that had taken his right eye, as well. The shrapnel had also embedded itself into the right side of his face, damaging the nerves and causing paralysis, which was why Hank was so good at that lopsided grin.

Despite all that, Hank was in amazing physical shape. He'd been fitted with a prosthetic leg, and the patch he wore over his right eye made him look like a rogue pirate, which the girls loved to tease him about. Hank had a great attitude and refused to let his losses define him as a person.

The sound of a current rock song coming out of the speakers in the main area of the bar told Clay that it was just about opening time. The digital entertainment system selected popular songs from a playlist and streamed the matching music videos onto the huge flat-screen TV on the far wall. It was a trendy, crowd-pleasing addition to the bar—something to watch, or you could join the action out on the dance floor, which usually ended up packed on ladies' night.

At four p.m., customers started arriving at Kincaid's, a gradual influx of men and women, most of whom arrived in groups of two or more. It started slowly enough that Samantha had the chance to learn the basics as she worked beside Amanda. Clay watched her take drink orders, sometimes asking Amanda a question before returning her attention to the customer. From what he could tell, she was picking up the bar terminology more quickly than he'd anticipated. She put in the orders and delivered the cocktails and bottles of beer on a serving tray with more coordination than he would have given her credit for.

For someone who'd grown up not having to work a day in her life, she appeared to be adapting well. Hell, she even seemed to be enjoying herself as she chatted with a group of women as she jotted down their drinks on a note pad. She moved on to the next table of young guys, who openly flirted with her. Clay's gut tied up in knots when she smiled back at them and laughed at something one of them said. He had to remind himself numerous times that pickup lines and casual advances were the nature of the beast in a place like this, and that all the bar waitresses got hit on on a regular basis. Hell, they even flirted back to increase their tips. As long as a customer wasn't crude and didn't make any physical sexual advances toward his girls, the behavior was tolerated.

But that mental lecture didn't stop Clay from glaring at some douchebag who was checking out Samantha's ass as she walked away to place the drink orders.

"Jesus, Clay. That scowl on your face is going to scare away customers," Katrina said as she slid onto a barstool in front of him.

He'd been so busy staring at Samantha he hadn't seen Katrina come in.

She followed his line of vision to the woman making him crazy in so many ways. "Or maybe that's your intention, to intimidate the hell out of every guy in the place so they don't touch your shiny new toy."

"She's not my anything," he said gruffly, wishing everyone would stop making that assumption. He shifted his gaze back to Katrina, surprised to see her at Kincaid's on a Monday evening. "What are you doing here, anyway? You never come in for ladies' night."

"That's because it's like a meat market out there," she said, wrinkling her nose in distaste as she indicated the crowd of men and women mingling. "You know everyone here is looking for a casual hookup, which is why I'm sitting *alone* at the bar."

Clay shrugged, though he knew she spoke the truth. "Not my business what they do once they leave the premises. I just serve the drinks while they're here, and you still didn't answer my question. Why are *you* here?"

"I'm providing moral support." She flashed him a grin.

"For Samantha?" he guessed as he refilled the garnish caddy with maraschino cherries.

Katrina nodded as she reached over and grabbed a stemmed fruit, then plucked the cherry off with her teeth and ate it. "Thought it might be nice for her to have a familiar face here tonight."

"I take it you two hit it off today while shopping?"

"Yeah." Katrina's expression softened. "She's actually really nice. For a rich girl."

He raised an inquisitive brow. The fact that Samantha's family owned a billion-dollar investment firm wasn't a piece of information he'd shared with Katrina, or anyone else. Maybe Samantha had told her, though he didn't think it likely, considering she was attempting to create a new life, away from the Jamieson wealth and influence.

"And you know she's rich based on what, exactly?" he asked.

Katrina rolled her eyes, as if it were obvious. "When I picked her up, she was carrying a three-thousand-dollar Louis Vuitton purse. At first, I thought it was a damned good knock-off, but when we walked into Target, she looked like a kid in a candy store. Although it was very cute how she tried to budget your money," she said with an amused grin. "Then, she seemed overwhelmed by all the shampoo and body wash choices and kept asking me what was the best product for the best price. A *normal* person would know exactly what they needed, and what brand to buy, because it's what they used on a regular basis."

It was clever and accurate deductive reasoning, but Clay didn't confirm or deny anything as he wiped down the service area. "Thanks again for taking her to the store and helping her to get what she needed," he said, and changed the subject. "Ladies' cocktails are half off tonight, so what can I get you to drink?"

"I'll take a mojito, please."

"Coming right up," he said, and tossed mint and lime into a glass so he could muddle it together before adding the alcohol.

Katrina turned in her chair, content to watch the activity going on around her from afar. The bar was starting to pick up and get much busier—which was normal by six in the evening, when everyone was done with their day jobs and wanted to take advantage of the half-price appetizers for happy hour. By seven, the place was usually packed and at the peak of activity.

After serving Katrina her drink, Clay continued working behind the bar, restocking items and helping Tara and Gina to keep up with the increasing rush of orders as more women arrived. The dance floor filled up, and the place became standing room only. At a little after seven, his brother Mason and a few of his friends walked into the joint, but Clay immediately lost sight of them as they blended into the crowd.

Undoubtedly, his brother was already working the women in the room, pouring on the charm and lining up his own *hit it and quit it* for the evening, which was Mason's method of operation when it came to females. And with his cocky, bad-boy persona, combined with his good looks and multitude of tattoos, he always had an abundance of willing females to choose from. And he never failed to take advantage of that fact.

Another half hour had passed when Tessa came up to the bar next to Katrina, not to collect a drink order but to get Clay's attention. She waved him over, her expression flushed and irritated.

"Everything okay?" Clay asked, immediately concerned.

"No." More irritation vibrated in her voice. "Your *brother* is in the women's restroom banging some chick, and I need to pee!"

He was so taken aback by her announcement that he frowned. "Mason?"

Katrina snorted, and it wasn't a pretty sound. "Who else would it be? Do you honestly think Levi would do something so indecent?"

Yeah, Katrina had a point. Only Mason would be so ballsy as to have sex in a semi-public place, while people waited to use the facilities. Ever since he was a teenager, his brother had developed an *I don't give a fuck* attitude that made him impulsive and careless, one that continued even now, at the age of twenty-seven. Mason had some of his shit together—he was a talented tattoo artist and owned his own shop—but their fucked-up childhood still affected him on an emotional level, and he dealt with all that painful shit in his own way. Namely by being reckless, wild, and pretending to be so aloof no one would even try to get close enough to crush him, the way their own mother had. Thus, his inclination toward one-night stands. Easy sex and no attachments. Ever.

Yeah, all three Kincaid brothers had mommy issues, and they each dealt with the residual effects in their own way. Growing up with a junkie for a mother who'd abandoned her kids for days at a time in order to get high, then had landed in prison for drug possession and prostitution, tended to leave a lasting impression on a kid. And that hadn't even been the

CARLY PHILLIPS & ERIKA WILDE

worst of what they'd gone through.

"Since Mason is ignoring me, can you *please* go and take care of the problem?" Tessa asked as she shifted uncomfortably on her feet.

*Problem* was too easy of a word for Mason. His brother was a pain in his ass. A thorn in his side. The shit on his shingle. There was nothing easy or predictable about Mason, and tonight's escapade proved as much.

Clay exhaled a harsh breath, but just as he tossed his damp rag behind the bar, intending to cut short Mason's fun, the man himself sauntered out of the crowd and headed toward the bar. By himself. But the arrogant swagger in his walk and the satisfied smile on his face definitely confirmed he'd just gotten lucky—and could easily get lucky again if he wanted to with one of the many females ogling him as he strolled by.

When he reached the end of the bar where they were gathered, relief flashed across Tessa's features. "It's about damn time, Romeo," she grumbled, and quickly beelined it for the ladies' room.

Mason merely smirked, which increased Clay's annoyance. "What the fuck are you doing in the *women's* restroom?"

"It's called getting laid," Mason replied as he slid onto the stool next to Katrina, who was frowning at Mason. "You should try it sometime, big brother. It might improve your testy mood and mellow you out some."

"My mood is fine," he snapped, unwilling to admit

just how much he *had* been on edge since that morning's hot, erotic kiss with Samantha. And watching her hustle around the place in those snug jeans and formfitting T-shirt wasn't helping his intense attraction to her, either. His dick had been at half-mast since she'd arrived at the bar, with no relief in sight.

But this wasn't about him. It was about Mason's behavior. "I don't appreciate you being so crass in my bar. If you were anyone else, I would have tossed you out on your ass."

"Luckily I'm in good with the owner." Mason grinned.

Clay reached into the bin of ice chilling the beers and pulled out a Sam Adams—his brother's drink of choice until he moved on to the harder stuff in an hour or so. "Not *that* good, so don't fucking press your luck." He removed the metal cap and set the bottle on the bar.

"Jesus, Mason," Katrina finally said, a sharp, chastising bite to her voice. "Can't you keep it in your pants for *one* night?"

Mason laughed at the obvious displeasure in her tone, and she visibly bristled. "Now why would I want to do that, Kitty-Kat?" he asked innocently, using the pet name he'd given her so many years ago.

"Oh, I don't know," she responded sarcastically. "So you don't catch something and your dick falls off?"

Her unflattering comment didn't even seem to faze him. "Not gonna happen. Condoms first, *always*," he said, and took a long drink of his beer.

Katrina made a distasteful sound in the back of her throat. "You're gross and disgusting."

"So you've told me many times before," Mason said, and suddenly grew more serious, which didn't happen often since being a smartass was more conducive to keeping most people at a distance. "But you're my very best friend, and I know deep down inside, you secretly love me despite my faults."

There was the slightest teasing note to Mason's voice that kept his reply from being too intimate, but the glimmer of something more briefly flashed in Katrina's eyes—a longing and desire that Clay had seen in her gaze before.

Jesus, his brother was a blind idiot for not seeing what was right in front of him, that the one woman who understood him better than he knew himself was his best friend. And she wanted more than the sibling-like relationship Mason had boxed her into.

Clay didn't know how his brother could be so obtuse, unless Mason deliberately kept Katrina squarely in the friend zone to protect his own emotions. Because if he didn't take that chance, there was no risk of being rejected or deserted, and that was something Clay identified with all too well.

Whatever had passed between Mason and Katrina was gone in the next instant, when Samantha came up to the service bar to *return* a drink order. Her face was flushed from rushing around, and she looked a bit frazzled by the fast-paced environment, as well as trying to learn on the fly.

"I'm so sorry, I punched in the wrong order again," she said with an apologetic grimace as she set a Tom Collins on the counter. "Who knew there were so many 'Collins' that a person can order? The guy wanted a *John* Collins," she clarified, sounding flustered and contrite. "I realize this is the fourth time I've ordered the wrong cocktail, and I know I'm wasting your profits since you can't resell the drinks. You can take the cost out of my paycheck."

Clay wanted to laugh, because one, she looked so damned cute, and two, money and making a profit wasn't a concern for him. But she didn't know that, and it wasn't something he made public. In fact, very few people—like a handful, and that included his brothers—knew just how wealthy he really was.

"Don't worry, Cupcake," he said, the endearment slipping past his lips much too easily before he could catch himself. "It's all part of the learning curve."

Clay grabbed a highball glass, filled it with ice, and reached for the bourbon.

Mason, who was sitting directly across from Clay and just a few feet away from Samantha, turned her way. Instantaneous interest lit up his blue eyes. "Cupcake?" he asked, presenting her with his most charming grin. "Is that your name? Because you look pretty damn sweet to me."

Katrina groaned and rolled her eyes.

Samantha laughed, and Clay was stupidly relieved when she didn't flirt back with Mason, something that didn't happen often with his brother. Those tribal tattoos covering his muscular arms were pretty much guaranteed to seduce most women, and those piercing sapphire eyes framed by thick black lashes usually had a woman's panties hitting the floor within seconds— just ask the girl Mason had just screwed in the bathroom.

"No, my name is Samantha," she said as she placed extra cocktail napkins on her tray. "Clay gave me the nickname of Cupcake because I'm a lightweight when it comes to drinking alcohol."

"Did he now?" Mason's gaze shifted to Clay, scrutinizing him as he raised a brow.

Oh, Clay knew that penetrating stare very well, the one that saw through many of his own defenses, as only a brother could. Before Mason said something inappropriate, Clay decided his best course of action would be to head Mason off at the pass with a change of subject and an introduction.

Clay garnished the fresh drink he'd just made with a lemon slice and set it on her tray. "Samantha, this is Mason. He's—"

"A *manwhore*," Katrina said tartly, cutting Clay off before he could say *brother*.

Samantha's eyes grew wide as she waited to see how Mason reacted to that. Obviously, Katrina was still miffed with him.

True to character, Mason didn't so much as flinch. Instead, he grinned, as if she'd just complimented him. "Be careful, Kitty-Kat," he said, leaning close enough so that when he spoke, his breath stirred against her blonde hair. "You're starting to sound jealous."

"I'm not jealous," Katrina insisted as she jerked away from him. "I'm just telling Samantha like it is so she keeps her distance. You, Mason Kincaid, are the male equivalent of a slut."

He put his hand over his heart and feigned a wounded look. "You say that like it's a *bad* thing."

Katrina just shook her head and let it go.

"It was nice meeting you, Mason," Samantha said as she picked up her tray, then made her way back into the throng of customers to deliver the new drink.

Mason turned his head and watched her the entire way, and Clay *knew* his brother's gaze was on her tight, curvy ass. He managed, just barely, to swallow the possessive growl that was trying to claw its way out of his throat. The last thing he needed was his brother homing in on the fact that Clay wanted Samantha for himself. Not that it was going to happen, but he wouldn't allow Mason to make a play for her, either.

Once Samantha disappeared from sight, Mason glanced back at Clay. "So, need some help breaking in the new bar waitress?" he asked wolfishly before finishing off the rest of his beer.

Clay glared at him, when he really wanted to punch his brother in the face. "Don't be an asshole, Mase."

"She's off-limits," Katrina suddenly announced. "She's living with Clay."

Mason's jaw dropped open in shock, and he snapped it shut again, his disbelief rendering him momentarily mute. After a few seconds passed, he shook his head at Clay. "What the fuck? Are you serious? Did you take in another stray and decide to keep her like you did Xena, *Saint Clay*?"

Clay clenched his jaw against Mason's sarcastic remark and sent Katrina a *thanks a fucking lot* glance before addressing his brother to tell him what he'd explained to everyone else so far. "It's temporary until she can find a place of her own, and before you ask, *no*, we're not hooking up."

"Too bad for you," Mason said in male sympathy, then he grinned like a rogue. "That's gotta be *hard*, letting her sleeping in your bed without you in it."

"Oh, you're 'punny'," he said of his brother's double entendre.

Mason slid off the barstool, obviously ready to move on to another form of entertainment. "I'll see you later, Kitty-Kat," he said to Katrina as he wound the purple-tipped ends of her hair around his finger to give it a playful tug. "And I might be in a little late tomorrow morning, depending on how my night ends." He winked at her.

"Not too late," she grumbled. "You have an eleven o'clock appointment with a woman who specifically asked for you. She wants a tattoo of a lock and key on the inside of each of her inner thighs."

Mason's gaze lit up. "Damn. I can already tell that tomorrow is going to be a great day since I'll be spending it between a woman's legs." And with that raunchy remark, he returned to what he did best…man-whoring.

Katrina expelled a deep sigh, the sound rife with fatigue that wasn't so much physical as it was emotional. "And that's why I don't come here on Monday nights," she said, reaching for her purse as she stood. "Your brother is here, and he drives me crazy for at least eight hours a day at the shop. No need to subject myself to any more torture than I've already put up with."

When she pulled out her wallet to pay, Clay waved away her attempt. "Your drink is on the house, and I'm sorry Mason can be such a dick sometimes." That, at least, got a smile out of her. "Have a good night, okay?"

She nodded. "Yeah, you, too."

# Chapter Six

B Y ELEVEN O'CLOCK that evening, when the bar finally closed for the night and all the customers were gone, Samantha looked like she'd been put through the wringer. Clay actually felt bad for her. Her face etched with exhaustion, she helped Tessa and Amanda clean the dirty glasses and plates from the tables, occasionally wincing as she bent over, then straightened again to put the items on her tray. Her back was obviously killing her.

He knew every inch of her body had to be tired and sore after working nonstop, but never once had she complained about the physical exertion. Hell, he'd hired other more experienced bar waitresses in the past who hadn't been able to handle the brisk, hectic, and fast pace at Kincaid's and had quit the first night. Not Samantha. She'd dealt incredibly well with the wide variety of people and the different personalities that she'd encountered over the course of the night.

Despite every snobby, pretentious stereotype he wanted to believe about a woman who was more a wealthy socialite than a blue-collar waitress, Samantha had proved to be incredibly friendly, engaging, and likeable. Everyone who worked at Kincaid's had already welcomed her into the fold and made her feel like one of the team, and they tended to be a tough crowd when it came to new hires.

The girls finished wiping down the tables and chairs, which was all Clay required them to do at the end of their shift. He had a crew who came in every morning to sweep and mop the floors, take out all the trash, and handle any other tedious chores so his employees could leave at a reasonable hour on a weekday. By eleven forty-five, everyone was gone except for him and Samantha, who plopped herself into a chair at one of the tables and let out a weary groan, as if she couldn't bring herself to move another inch.

He came around the bar, wanting to check on her. "Are you all right?"

"No." She grimaced as she arched her spine to stretch her back muscles, which effectively thrust her breasts out and drew his stare to her stiff nipples poking against the cotton fabric of her T-shirt. "I feel like I have a hangover and I didn't even drink anything tonight. And my feet are killing me. Oh, and I'm starving."

Reluctantly dragging his gaze from her chest, he

thought about the one piece of toast she'd had this morning for breakfast and wondered if she'd eaten anything since. "Did you have lunch before starting your shift?"

"I had a burger at a fast-food place with Katrina after we went shopping, but that was almost nine hours ago." A small smile quirked the corner of her mouth. "Damn, I burned a lot of calories tonight running around, and my stomach has been growling hungrily for the past two hours."

He frowned at her. "You should have taken a break and ordered something from the kitchen. All employees eat during their shift at no charge." He shook his head as that natural inclination to take care of her surfaced. "Stay here. I'll be right back."

"As if I could even move now that I'm sitting down," she said as she absently rubbed a hand along the back of her neck and moaned as she kneaded the taut tendons there. It was all he could do not to push her hands away and take over himself, easing the knots out of her sore muscles. "I might just sleep right here with my head on the table," she added.

Resisting the continuing urge to take over and give her a relaxing massage himself—*any excuse to touch her again*—he went to the kitchen, which was a much safer option. He heated up a few appetizers in the micro-wave and grabbed a small bottle of water from the refrigerator.

When he returned to the table, she was counting out the tips she'd made, and had created two separate stacks of dollar bills.

"Here, you need to eat," he said, setting the plate of food and drink to the side before taking the chair across from her.

"Thank you. I will in a minute," she replied, her focus on the task in front of her. "I just want to get this counted out."

He leaned back in his seat, enjoying the quiet moment of just watching her. Her brows were furrowed in concentration, and when she absently bit her bottom lip, a distinct heat pooled low in his belly. This morning's memory of how she'd brazenly nipped at his own lip and tugged it between her teeth flooded his mind, followed by the sweet taste of her mouth and her uninhibited response to his aggressive kiss.

He wanted to kiss her again. Badly. Hell, if he was completely honest with himself, what he really craved was the feel of her soft, curvy body straining beneath his as he held her down and drove his cock hard and deep inside her, claiming her completely. He ached to wrap his hands tight in her hair and hear her whimper and moan and beg for him to give her the release she so desperately needed. And he'd make damn sure she came long and hard, until she was weak and sated and sore in the best way possible so she'd forget every pansy-ass bastard who'd come before him.

His cock pulsed at the erotic fantasy playing in his head, and he shifted in his chair. He'd never had such an instantaneous attraction to a woman as he did now with Samantha. And he'd never had to struggle so much to keep such a tight rein on his desires. Samantha made him want to *lose* control, in her and with her, and that scared the crap out of him because it would lead to complications...and the kind of strings he didn't allow in his life.

"I had no idea what to expect tip-wise since I've never done this before, but this is way more than I'd anticipated," she said, drawing him out of his private thoughts.

A hint of pride threaded through her voice, and she pushed the larger bundle of cash across the table toward him. "Here's part of what I owe you for the clothing and toiletries I bought today. I kept a little bit for myself for incidentals, but if I do this well every night, I should have you paid off in a few days, and then I can start saving up for another place to stay and be out of your way."

He opened his mouth to say he didn't mind her being there, then closed it before the words could come out. *What the hell?* How was it that in just *one day* he'd become attached to her and didn't want her to leave? Jesus, he was so fucked.

"You did well tonight," he said instead, indicating the money she'd made.

She gave him a smile, and there was no mistaking the gleam of satisfaction in her eyes. "You sound surprised."

"Maybe because I am," he admitted with a shrug. "You picked things up pretty quickly for not having any experience."

She tucked the smaller amount of money back into the pouch in her waitress apron, then moved the plate of food so that it was in front of her. "Just because I'm blonde doesn't mean I'm ditzy," she teased as she picked up a potato skin loaded with melted cheese, bacon, and sour cream. "I'll have you know I graduated summa cum laude from Northwestern University with a degree in political science."

He watched her polish off the appetizer in two hungry bites, appropriately impressed by her education. He knew she wasn't bragging, just stating that she wasn't a slouch. Not that he'd ever thought she was, nor had he doubted her competence. She was beautiful and a billionaire heiress, but in the short time he'd known her, he'd already come to the conclusion that she was also intelligent, not to mention a woman who prided herself on being independent—something she apparently hadn't been allowed while living at home.

Curious, he asked, "So what have you used that fancy, illustrious degree for?"

She finished off a chicken finger, the lighthearted glow in her eyes dimming at his question. "Nothing," she said quietly. "I attended a private university because that's what had been laid out for me, and paid for, since I was child. I didn't have a choice in the matter. I went with political science to challenge myself and because government and world events interest me. I thought about going to law school, but my parents nixed that idea. Allowing me to pursue any ambition might have hampered their plans for me to marry well. And soon." She drew a deep breath. "In the end, the degree was all for show, and my parents were able to brag about the fact that I graduated at a prestigious university with the highest honors."

"You wanted to go to law school?" he asked, surprised once again.

She shook her head. "In the end…no. I think I wanted to have something for me. But that wasn't allowed. After all, what did I need a further degree for when I was expected to get married, be some man's arm candy, and stay home and have babies?" Her voice dipped lower, a hint of disgust in her tone.

He raised a brow. "You don't want to get married and have a family?"

"Of course I do," she replied indignantly. "With a man who *I* fall in love with, not one who is handpicked for me. But I want, and need, more out of my life than being married to a man for business reasons and to secure my father's company."

That, he could understand. And he respected her for being strong enough to stand by her convictions, which obviously meant defying her parents. "I get your need to be self-sufficient, but I'm sure you don't want to be a waitress for the rest of your life."

She took a drink from her water bottle, her eyes dancing with humor as she swallowed the cool liquid, then finally said, "You have to admit, it's an interesting start to whatever comes next."

He chuckled, appreciating her positive attitude. "If you could do anything *you* wanted, what would you do?" He didn't know why he asked the question, or why he even cared what she envisioned for her future, but everything about this woman intrigued him and he found himself invested despite all the warnings he'd given himself since the second they'd met.

"Well...even though my degree is in political science, I've since realized I have no interest in being involved in politics or being a lawyer or working in public relations." Finished with the snack he'd made for her, she pushed the plate aside and crossed her arms over the surface of the table, her gaze meeting his almost shyly. "What I would love to do is be a pastry chef."

He couldn't have been more shocked and leaned forward in his seat. "Really?"

She nodded eagerly, clearly warming to the topic. "When I was growing up, I'd always sneak into the kitchen and help our housekeeper, Maggie, when she was making desserts," she said with an impish smile. "She taught me all about baking cakes and pastries and pies, and I loved working with her. My mother just thought it was a phase I was going through, and since being with Maggie in the kitchen kept me busy and out of her way, she allowed me to spend time with the help." She wrinkled her nose in an adorable fashion. "Two years ago, I went to culinary school to get certified as a pastry chef, but again, my parents didn't take it seriously."

"But you did go," he said quietly.

She nodded, a glint of pride and defiance in her

pretty eyes.

Without really thinking about the implications of his actions, he reached a hand across the table and slid it on top of one of hers, telling himself it was a gesture of silent support and encouragement. And not because he ached to touch her. "If it makes you happy, you should do it."

She exhaled a sigh and turned her hand over beneath the weight of his, so that her fingers brushed against his sensitive palm, making that connection between them so much stronger...and seductive, letting him know they were both feeling the underlying desire arcing between them. And though they'd been fighting those emotions—or at least he was—with every passing minute, she was getting harder and harder to resist.

"I've seriously thought about it," she revealed, and he realized she was talking about becoming a pastry chef and not the desire that was building by the minute. "But here I am, twenty-six years old with no real life or job experience as a pastry chef, or anything else, for that matter. I'm not sure any one-star restaurant would even give me a chance, never mind a five-star establishment."

He heard the insecurities in her voice, and self-doubt wasn't something he'd equate with the woman sitting in front of him. "You won't know unless you try." He didn't want to see her give up on her dreams.

She possessed so many fascinating layers. So much emotional depth. And every time they really talked, he learned things about Samantha that changed his entire perspective of her, in a way that was dangerous to the safe life he'd carved out for himself until now.

Realizing how intimate touching her hand had become, he pulled his arm back to his side of the table.

She dipped her head self-consciously and abruptly changed the subject. "What about you? How did you come to own a bar?"

He reclined in his chair, thinking for a moment before answering. He wasn't sure how much he wanted to reveal about his disturbing and hellish childhood and the ensuing teenage years, so he decided to go with the abbreviated, uncomplicated version.

"Jerry, the guy who originally owned this bar, hired me when I was sixteen and in desperate need of a job." Because he'd had two younger brothers to feed, clothe, and make sure they had a roof over their heads. "I started out sweeping the floors, emptying the trash, and doing general cleanup. I worked my ass off, and he became a father figure to me, since I didn't have one. The harder I worked, the more he taught me about the bar and business, and the more responsibilities he gave me. When I turned twenty-one, he put me behind the bar and trained me to be a bartender and how to make drinks. He was kind and caring and selfless when it came to helping other people."

"You said 'was,'" she stated softly.

Clay felt his chest tighten as it always did when he recalled how devastated he'd been on finding Jerry's lifeless body in the office that fateful day. "He had a heart attack and passed away when I was twenty-four. And that's when I found out he left the bar to me. He had no wife, no family, and no kids."

And along with the establishment, Clay had inherited the small fortune that Jerry had amassed—a shocking two million dollars that the older man had hoarded away and Clay hadn't known existed. Other than sharing part of the wealth with his brothers, he'd kept most of it invested and used some of the extra money to help his employees when needed. Like Tara and college. She still didn't know that he'd been the one to cover her entire tuition, and believed she'd been awarded a grant by an anonymous donor. And he'd done the same thing with Hank's medical bills— paid them off in full without disclosing his identity.

He didn't miss the irony—Mason called him Saint Clay, and maybe he was a bit of an altruist—but Clay didn't do it because he wanted the recognition or praise. He did it because he knew how it felt to struggle under the weight of financial burden and trying to make it on your own. Or in his case, with two brothers he'd been determined wouldn't end up in foster care. And now that he had the means, he wanted to lighten the strain for those he cared about.

Samantha tipped her head, her blue eyes analyzing him in a way that seemed to see right past those walls he erected to keep people out. He could *feel* her penetrating stare, see the discerning look in her gaze, and that sudden connection between them unnerved him.

"Katrina was right, you know," she finally said, breaking the silence that had settled over the room. "You're very different from your brother Mason."

Abrupt laughter escaped him, because that was the last thing he'd expected her to say. But he was grateful to know that she saw him differently from his wild and unpredictable sibling. "Thank God I'm *not* like Mason," he said, then leaned forward in his chair and addressed the first part of her comment. "What, exactly, did Katrina tell you about me?"

"That you're the responsible one," she replied, and propped her chin in her hand. "Why do people call you Saint?"

"That nickname came from Mason," he said wryly, and his sibling meant it in a purely mocking way. If you asked his brother why he called Clay *Saint*, he'd say because Clay was a do-gooder, which was the complete opposite of Mason's cocky, *I don't give a shit* attitude. "He calls me a saint because I tend to give people a chance."

"Like Hank and Elijah?" she asked perceptively. "And me," she added more appreciatively.

"Yes." There was no sense in denying the truth. "I didn't have the best life before Jerry hired me, and I'm fortunate enough that I'm now in the position that I can help other people who need it. Even if that means giving them something as simple as a job."

She smiled at him. "I love that you see the good in people."

"It wasn't always that way," he replied gruffly. No,

for the longest time, he'd painted people with the same brush as his mother and the man who'd fathered him, believing the worst of the world and the people who inhabited it. Neglect along with physical and emotional abuse were all he'd known for his entire childhood, and judging people and their intentions had been a hard habit for him to break. Trusting them had been equally difficult for him. Until Jerry. The man had broken through his anger and reserve in a way no one else ever had, teaching him to at least give people the benefit of the doubt.

"Your life is so completely opposite from how I grew up," Samantha said, breaking into his thoughts. "Everything was just handed to me on a proverbial silver platter, and I took things for granted." She ducked her head in embarrassment before meeting his gaze. "It's just that…"

The sadness clouding her gaze made him want to know more, because whatever she had to say suddenly mattered to him. "What?"

She gave a one-shoulder shrug. "The world I lived in, it's all so superficial, and I felt like I was suffocating. With Harrison, too. But every time I wanted to do something for me, to better myself or make a difference in my own life, I'd be reminded that I'm a Jamieson, and I had certain expectations I had to live up to. What I wanted didn't matter."

"Well, look at you now," he said on a teasing drawl, meant to lighten the mood. "All stubborn and rebellious."

"Yeah, and it feels good, *really good*, not to have to worry about what my parents think, and whether or not they'd approve of what I do." A sexy, brazen smile curved her lips, and her eyes glinted with the kind of simmering desire that made Clay's body heat in an answering awareness.

"I think I like being a bad girl," she said huskily. "It's quite liberating."

Confession out in the open, she pushed up from the table, and Clay quickly realized that trouble was heading his way. She took the few steps toward him, hips swaying in a confident, alluring manner, before she plopped herself in his lap like a tempting present he didn't want to return and couldn't wait to unwrap.

Her perfect ass nestled right up against his groin, and his entire body stiffened, including his dick. She sat sideways on his hard thighs, and it took Herculean strength not to swivel her around and reposition her so she was straddling his hips. He wanted nothing more than to rock his thickening shaft between her jean-clad legs. As it was, keeping his arms at his sides and his hands off any part of her body was testing his normally solid restraint.

She had no such qualms and grabbed his wrist, lifted his hand, and settled his palm on the curve of her hip. Dark blue eyes locked on his, the depths swirling with the same need pounding relentlessly through him. "Touch me, Clay," she invited in a soft, sultry whisper.

His fingers tightened on her waist in a desperate attempt to keep his hand from sliding beneath her T-shirt and up to caress her full breasts. "*Samantha*," he groaned, his voice a low and rough discouragement. "I already warned you this morning—"

"That you aren't a gentleman and you don't do soft and gentle and sweet," she said, repeating the exact words he'd uttered as she placed her hand on his chest, her touch searing him even through the cotton fabric of his T-shirt.

"But I don't need or want a warning, Clay. All day long I've been thinking about the things you said, about the things you want to do to me, and asking myself if that's what I want, too."

*I like to control and fuck so hard and deep you'll scream and be sore the next day. I'd want you on your knees, with my hands fisted in your hair while you suck my cock, and then I'd bend you over this table, spread your legs wide, and fuck you all over again.*

And that was just to start with. From there, it would only get hotter. Dirtier. Those filthy thoughts and fantasies made his blood boil in his veins. "You have no idea what you want," he tried warning her again.

"Now that's where you're wrong," she said seductively as she slid her hand up to his neck and stroked her thumb along the pulse he could feel throbbing at the base of his throat. "I know, without a doubt, that I want *you*. More than I've ever wanted another man."

The truth of that statement blazed in her eyes, scorching hot and fiery. Her admission pushed him closer to his breaking point and made his cock so hard it ached. "I'm trying like hell not to take advantage of what you're offering, but a man can only take so much."

She dipped her head to the other side of his neck, her soft laughter warm and damp against his skin. "That's what I'm counting on," she said into his ear. "I've had enough of soft and easy and romantic with other guys, and especially Harrison, who won't even touch me between my legs because he's obsessed with cleanliness and doesn't like anything on his fingers or hands."

*What the fuck?* Clay thought, trying to wrap his mind around what she'd just said, but she wasn't done destroying his sanity.

"That kiss this morning with you...just thinking about it and all the things you said to me, about how you want to take me hard and deep and how you want me on my knees while I...suck your cock, it makes me..."

"Wet?" he suggested when she seemed unable to finish her sentence. God, he ought to be putting an end to her seduction, not encouraging her to continue!

She rubbed her legs together restlessly, as if to confirm what he'd suggested, and the way she shifted on his lap made him impossibly harder against her ass.

"That's definitely one of the things," she said, her amused voice tickling his ear. "But it also makes me want so much more. Like to know what it would feel like to have your mouth on me and your tongue giving me pleasure. Or what you would feel like sliding deep inside of me."

She sounded so prim and proper, when he was dying to hear dirtier, more shocking words fall from her lips. Like what it would feel like to have him eat her pussy like he was starving and suck her clit into his mouth until she came on his tongue. Or what it would be like to have his cock driving into her tight heat as he fucked her until she splintered apart and screamed his name. But good girls didn't do or say things like that—

"I don't want to be a good girl anymore," she said, somehow so in tune to him she'd read his mind. Pressing her lips against his neck, she licked his skin with her soft tongue, making him shudder with the need to feel her mouth and tongue stroking along his dick. "I want to be very bad with you, *Saint* Clay."

Breathing hard, he lifted his hand and twisted his fingers into her hair, then tugged her head back so he was looking into her eyes, which were so dark and dilated he wanted to drown in all that sweet sensuality.

"I'm not a *saint*, Cupcake," he said, even as he felt himself caving in to his own desperate hunger for this one woman alone. "*Especially* when it comes to fucking."

"That's good, because I don't really want a saint," she taunted softly, as she dragged her tongue across her bottom lip, then smiled sensuously. "I want a *sinner*."

Just like this morning, she managed to provoke him past the point of no return. *How did she manage that when no other woman ever could?*

Her lashes fell to half-mast, and she parted those full pink lips, already breathless and flushed at the mere thought of him kissing her again. Fuck trying to be honorable, he thought, as the last of his self-discipline evaporated and his aggressive side surfaced.

If she wanted a sinner, well, sinning was what he did best.

Tightening his hold on her hair, he tipped her head to the side and didn't hesitate to claim her mouth—hard, deep, and thoroughly. Just like he ached to claim her body.

But *that* wasn't going to happen, so this kiss would have to suffice.

He swallowed her initial gasp and swirled his tongue over and around hers, dragging her further into his kind of debauchery. Her soft, supple mouth was made for sex and sin, *and for sucking his cock*, he thought with a fevered groan. Her flavor was deliciously addicting, and he knew kissing her would never be enough to quench this never-ending desire, or to sate the lust that threatened to consume him. But it *had* to be enough, because anything more would ruin her.

He didn't do promises. He didn't do love or forever. He was dark, and she was light. She was pure, and he was tainted and majorly fucked up. And she deserved so much more than he could ever offer her.

So for the second time in the same day, he was going to turn down a sure thing. *Jesus, when did I become so fucking chivalrous?* He told himself he didn't want

Samantha to have regrets, but what he really feared was that once he knew what it felt like to be buried deep inside of her, he'd never want to let her go.

He ended the kiss, and a needy moan escaped her lips as she opened her eyes. He ignored the clear disappointment in her gaze and the throbbing ache in his balls. "It's late, Samantha," he said. As an excuse, it was a pitiful one.

Surprisingly, she didn't argue. "It *is* late, and I need a long, hot shower." She slid off his lap and stood but held his gaze as a slow, daring smile touched her kiss-swollen lips. "Are you coming up?"

There was no mistaking the invitation in her words, but he shook his head and held firm, because he already knew how tempting it was to share a shower with her, and tonight she was completely sober. "No. Not for a while."

Amusement etched her features, even as she pinned him with a gutsy look. "Afraid I'll try and have my wicked way with you?"

"Not at all." No, he was more afraid that he'd corner her like a lust-crazed animal and finish what they'd started. It wasn't as though she was putting up any kind of struggle, and he honestly didn't know how much longer he could turn down her advances.

"Okay then," she said with an easy shrug and a too-knowing smile, clearly not believing him for a second. "Good night, *Saint*."

Yeah, she was mocking him with the nickname, so he did the same. "Good night, *Cupcake*."

She laughed, the lighthearted sound making him smile as she walked away, leaving him to wonder what her next plan of attack would be. And whether he'd have the strength and fortitude to resist.

# Chapter Seven

SAMANTHA CLOSED THE hardcover novel she was reading—a current best seller that had been lying on the coffee table—and exhaled a frustrated sigh. Three long days had passed since the night in the bar with Clay, and he'd made himself deliberately scarce ever since. He was gone when she woke up in the morning, and he remained downstairs long after closing while she returned to the apartment alone. For all she knew, he slept downstairs at the bar, as well.

Clearly, he was avoiding being alone with her, but that didn't change the sexual pull between them, which was obvious and glaring when she saw him during her shift. Even when they were in the crowded bar, surrounded by dozens of people, she'd catch him watching her with those dark brown eyes—not as her *employer* but as a hot-blooded man who wanted to ravish her.

The thought made her shiver, especially since she'd already had a sampling of Clay's seductive kisses, which were so delicious they became habit forming. And just like a junkie hooked on opiates, she craved more of him, her body constantly on edge with desire and the need to experience every last sensation he generated. He was her drug of choice, and withdrawals were starting to settle in and make her restless.

Standing up, she made her way into the kitchen in Clay's apartment and poured herself a small glass of apple juice. It was only eleven o'clock in the morning, and she was bored. Over the past few days, she'd managed to keep herself busy until her shift started. She'd cleaned up Clay's place and used some of her tip money to replenish the basics in his refrigerator—milk, bread, butter, some protein and fruits and vegetables so they'd have things to eat. She did his laundry, and one morning she'd strolled the neighborhood to familiarize herself with the area and the nearby businesses.

She'd found a family-owned grocery store, an Italian restaurant, and even a trendy boutique called Dress For Less, where she'd purchased a few cute outfits, a pretty matching lacy bra and panty set, and sandals all for less than fifty bucks. Another afternoon, she'd looked up the name and address of Mason's tattoo shop on Clay's laptop, and using MapQuest for directions, she'd walked the city block to Inked and checked out the place. Katrina had been sitting at the receptionist's desk and greeted her with a friendly, welcoming smile. She'd even taken a break so they could get an iced coffee and chat for a bit about the frustrating men in their lives—Mason and Clay.

After much deliberation, Samantha had decided to send her mother a postcard with a brief note, just so her parents would know that she was okay and her choice to not come home was a deliberate one. She didn't want their input or interference when it came to her decisions about what she would do with her life and future. She was still trying to figure that out. But the more she thought back on her conversation with Clay about her desire to be a pastry chef, the more the idea appealed to her. He hadn't laughed at her, which only fueled her determination to *try*. She just wished she wasn't so self-conscious about her lack of experience, the one main obstacle that caused her to hesitate in pursuing her dream job.

Today, though, she was out of ideas to keep herself busy. She finished off the chilled apple juice just as she felt a soft stroke of fur brush against her ankle. She glanced down and found Xena looking up at her with her one good eye and meowing softly. Smiling, Samantha picked up the sweet, loving cat and cuddled the feline against her chest, remembering the story Clay had told her about how he'd rescued the kitten when most people wouldn't have saved her based on her mangy appearance and vet expenses.

"Your owner is a softy, you know that?" Samantha asked as she scratched Xena behind an ear, and grinned when the cat purred in agreement. "He's also stubborn and hardheaded, gorgeous, and so freakin' hot he drives me crazy," she grumbled in exasperation.

As if commiserating, Xena rubbed her head against Samantha's palm, shamelessly demanding the attention and affection she wanted.

*That's exactly what I need to do*, Samantha suddenly realized with clarity—make her desires known and demand what she wanted, without taking no for an answer. There was no question that Clay was equally hot for her. One of them had to push past that steadfast control of his, and she knew it had to be her.

She shivered at the prospect of satisfying the sexual hunger between them, but, she admitted to herself, she hoped to gain more than just sex with Clay. She wanted an intimate glimpse into the man he really was. Based on what Katrina had told her and the few things Clay had shared, she already knew he'd had a rough life, and he quite obviously kept people at a distance because of it.

She ached to discover everything about the man. She'd glimpsed those darker shadows in his eyes when he'd talked about his past and told her about Jerry, the father figure in his life. What had happened to his real dad? As the oldest of three siblings, and clearly the responsible one, she suspected he'd taken on that role for his brothers. And what about his mother? Where was she now? Samantha wanted to know all that and more.

But right now, she'd settle for seducing him. Finally breaking down those physical barriers and experiencing the hot, dirty, sexual encounter he'd threatened her with in an effort to scare her away. Too bad for Clay, the new and emboldened Samantha Jamieson didn't frighten easily.

She was in this for the long haul, whether Clay liked it...or not.

CLAY WAS BECOMING a Tetris champion and not by choice. No, he was playing the online game on his office computer as a way to pass the hours until his employees arrived. Normally, he'd be upstairs, taking a break and relaxing before the bar opened, but he'd deemed the place off-limits while Samantha was up there during the day.

As a result of his self-imposed isolation, he'd never been so caught up on inventory, payroll, and scheduling. His office was cleaner than it had been in months, and all the paperwork that normally piled up on his desk was cleared off and filed, all invoices paid, compliance reports signed and submitted. He had nothing left to do during the day, so Tetris had become his best friend.

He just didn't trust himself to be alone with Samantha and not do something incredibly stupid, like touch her, or kiss her *again*, which would undoubtedly lead to stripping her naked and slaking the lust that smoldered just below the surface.

At every opportunity, Samantha tempted him, and

he knew if he allowed his control to slip any further, things between them would get down and dirty, and very quickly. Every man had a breaking point when it came to sex, and he was inches away from his. There would be no stopping the inevitable, and once he was deep inside her, he'd dominate her pleasure, dictate her release, and own her body. He physically shook at the thought of possessing this woman, and a low, tormented groan escaped his throat.

But the visual didn't stop there, as the scene played out in his mind. He'd fucking demand everything she had to give, and steal even more, until she was too wasted to even think or move. Then he'd take her all over again. Harder. Faster. Deeper. That was the illicit fantasy that kept him tossing and turning on the couch all night long, his dick rock hard and throbbing for relief. Just as it was right now, he thought as he rubbed his palm over the growing bulge in his pants.

"Need some help with that?" a husky, feminine voice asked.

His eyes snapped back open. For a moment, he thought he was hallucinating Samantha as a residual effect of the fantasy that he'd just entertained, but when she shut the office door and locked it behind her, he knew this woman was no figment of his imagination.

He also knew the moment of reckoning had arrived, and he sat up straighter in his chair, wondering if his dwindling willpower had any chance against the determination shining in her eyes or the purposeful way she strolled toward his desk.

He didn't know if she'd dressed for seduction, but the outfit she wore did it for him in a major way. A pale yellow lace top, cropped just above her waist, exposed the soft, creamy skin of her stomach, and a matching layered lace skirt that ended mid-thigh showed off her long, sexy legs. Her silky blonde hair fell in soft waves around her shoulders, and as she closed the distance between them, he grew dizzy, as if all the air had suddenly been sucked out of the room.

She came around the desk and stopped right between his spread thighs. Close enough for him to reach out and stroke his fingers along the bare flesh of her abdomen or down her long, sleek legs. Or, if he leaned forward, he could easily dip and swirl his tongue into her navel. Just the thought had his mouth watering for a taste.

With effort, he kept his hands and mouth to himself and dragged his gaze back up to her face. There was no missing the seductive smile on her pink, glossy lips or the naughty intentions flickering in her gaze. He was so screwed.

"How long do you intend to avoid being alone with me?" she asked, tipping her head to the side as she asked the question.

*As long as possible*, he wanted to say, except it didn't escape his notice that he was alone with her now, so it was a moot point. And she knew it, too.

"It's for your own good," he said gruffly.

"Why is it that everyone else thinks they know

what's best for me?" A small frown formed between her brows. "When does what *I* want matter?"

He heard the annoyance in her voice, and even understood her frustration, but that didn't stop him from trying *one more time* to dissuade her. "Samantha—"

"Please don't say no," she pleaded softly as she skimmed the tips of her fingers along his hard thigh, which sent a shaft of heat straight up to his already aching cock. "Not this time. I'm a grown woman, Clay, and I want you. And I know you feel the same way." Her blue eyes shimmered with determination.

That same determination that kept her on the wrong side of town despite what her family wanted. She was a strong woman, despite having let herself be led down a path that was clearly wrong for her. She'd decided the time had come to take what she wanted from life. And she wanted him.

He clenched his jaw, his good intentions wavering as she leaned in closer. "You're eating me up with those dark eyes right now, and even though you haven't touched me yet, I'm getting wet at the thought of all the dirty things you want to do to me." She slid her tongue along her full lips. "Not to mention all the things I've thought about doing to you."

*Oh, fuck me*, he thought as the last of his self-control crumbled to dust. She'd become so bold and brazen since the first night he'd seen her sitting at his bar. In such a short time, she'd blossomed into a sensual, confident woman who wasn't afraid to go after what she desired, so why was he denying them both the intense, heated pleasure they craved?

He could no longer answer that question, and at the moment, with her bracing her hands on his thighs and slowly lowering herself so that she was kneeling between his legs, his reasons no longer mattered.

"Take off your shirt so I can touch you," she said softly, huskily, her guileless blue eyes encouraging him.

He immediately pulled his shirt over his head and let it drop to the floor. She stared in awe at his bare chest, her fingers tightening on his denim-clad thighs as her gaze traveled all the way down to the thick length of his shaft straining against the fly of his jeans. He was hard as fuck for her.

Circling his fingers around her slender wrists, he guided both her hands up and placed them flat on his bare chest. Her palms were cool on his feverish skin, and the erotic contrast made him grit his teeth against the instinctive urge to take control of the situation, along with the woman who was making him *feel* so much more than just lust.

*Soon*, he told himself. But the next few minutes were for her. "Touch all you want, because once you're done, *I'm* going to be in charge, do you understand?"

She nodded jerkily, and he released her wrists, giving her time to explore his body. Her teeth sank into her lush bottom lip as she reverently slid her hands over the muscular planes of his chest and down his rib cage, using her thumbs to trace the definition of his abs until she reached his jeans.

Hooking her fingers into the waistband, she looked up at him with a wicked gleam in her eyes. "You're so hard and hot..." she murmured as she leaned forward and licked a slow, sinuous path along his stomach with her soft, wet tongue. "And *salty.*"

A tremor passed through him, and he hissed out a breath, suddenly desperate to feel that beautiful, tempting mouth on his cock. Done letting her play, he tunneled the fingers of one hand tightly into her hair, making sure she knew and understood that he was now calling the shots.

Excitement brightened her gaze, and he knew they were on the same page.

"Unzip my pants and release my dick."

Eagerly, she did as he demanded. When she had the fly of his jeans spread open, she grabbed the waistband and briefs and pulled them both down his hips, until his shaft was freed. His solid erection pulsed with need, and he circled his fingers around the firm length, slowly stroking his rigid flesh. She watched with a combination of fascination and dark, wild excitement. A drop of pre-cum seeped from the tip, and he dragged the pad of his thumb across the sensitive head, coating his finger with the sticky fluid.

Curious to see how far she was willing to go and how adventurous she would be, he pressed his slick thumb into her mouth so she could taste him. "You know what I want, don't you, sweetheart?"

Dreamy eyes locked on his. She didn't hesitate to close her lips around the finger, her tongue lapping around the digit and her teeth grazing his knuckle as she answered in actions, not words.

Oh, yeah, she knew *exactly* what was playing through his mind.

He withdrew his thumb from her warm, luscious mouth, already imagining filling it back up with his pulsing shaft. "Tell me what I want you to do with your soft, hot mouth," he coaxed in a low, rough voice.

The enticing flush of anticipation swept across her cheeks. "You want me to suck your cock."

Hearing his sweet cupcake speak those dirty words ramped up his lust even more. "Fuck yeah. I've been dying to feel your lips sliding down my cock. I've fantasized about it and jacked off in the shower with those images in my head." *Numerous times.*

"Then let me," she begged breathlessly. "Please."

Done teasing them both, he wound the long strands of her hair around his fist, so tight and secure there would be no doubt in her mind who had the upper hand. That her mouth was his to do with as he pleased.

He guided her head forward, pushed his cock between her parted lips, and didn't stop until the sensitive crest bumped against the back of her throat. She didn't jerk back. Didn't push away from him. Instead, her lashes fluttered closed and she moaned, the sound vibrating along his shaft and tightening his balls.

*Jesus fucking Christ.* His body shook like it was his

first time getting a blow job, and it took every ounce of willpower he possessed not to thrust his hips and fuck her perfect mouth harder, deeper. As it was, surrounded by all that silky heat and feeling the suctioning pull on his cock as he slowly drew her back up the length of his shaft, he suspected he was only going to last a few strokes.

She went down on him again, her greedy, hungry lips and tongue wreaking havoc with every last semblance of his control and shoving him closer to orgasm. The scrape of her fingernails down his flexing abdomen added to the erotic sensations surging through him, and when she opened her lashes and looked up at him with passion-blurred eyes that told him how much she loved sucking his cock, he was done for.

Breathing fast and feeling the rush of adrenaline in his veins warning him of his impending climax, he loosened his hold on her hair, giving her room to release him. "I'm going to fucking come, Samantha. *Hard*," he rasped, barely recognizing his own gravelly voice. "If you don't want that, you need to stop. *Now*."

She ignored his warning and took him to the back of her throat again and swallowed, the tight muscles there squeezing around the head and triggering the hottest, fiercest orgasm he'd ever had. The muscles in his stomach contracted, and he came on a hoarse shout, his hips jerking while her mouth continued to devastate him. Feeling as though he'd just been through a major hurricane, he dropped his head back against his chair and squeezed his eyes shut, trying to recover from the tempestuous storm that was Samantha.

It took a few minutes for his heart to stop racing and his breathing to return to normal, and when he finally opened his eyes again, he found her still kneeling on the floor in front of him, a pleased smile on her lips. And she had every right to be delighted with herself, because she'd just ruined him for any other woman.

Instead of dwelling on the implication of that unsettling thought, he focused his attention on making sure that he returned the favor and that Samantha was equally satisfied. Especially when he thought about what she'd told him about her ex, that he wouldn't touch her between her legs because he was a germ freak. Before they were done, Clay was not only going to touch her soft, wet pussy with his fingers, he would lap up her delectable juices with his tongue and make sure every inch of his cock was covered in all that slick moisture while making her come as hard as he had.

"Stand up," he said, back in control again.

Her eyes widened at the authoritative tone of his voice, but she quickly scrambled to her feet in front of him. He met her bright, anxious gaze and sat forward in his chair, his pants still undone. Keeping his eyes locked on hers, he lifted his hand and skimmed his fingers up the inside of one quivering thigh. His hand disappeared beneath the hem of her short skirt, traveling up, up, up, until he reached the silky barrier of her panties.

He pressed two fingers against the heated crotch of her underwear, which was soaked through with arousal—all from sucking him off. "You're fucking drenched," he murmured. He lightly rubbed her through the wet fabric, loving the helpless little sounds she made in the back of her throat. "And you're needy, too, aren't you?"

"Yes. So needy," she whispered almost desperately as she pushed her hips toward his hand, trying to increase the pressure of his fingers against that sweet spot he'd yet to truly focus on. "I need to come so badly."

"Don't worry, I promise we'll get there." His face was now level with her stomach, and he skimmed his mouth along the bare skin there, licking the sensitive patch of flesh below her navel, just like she'd done to him.

She moaned and shifted anxiously on her feet. "Clay…" she implored softly.

Not yet ready to ease her ache, he ignored her needy plea and slid her panties off, letting them drop to the floor, a pile of wet silk at her feet. She stepped out of them, pushing them aside.

He eased his hands around to the backs of her knees and slowly glided his palms up her thighs, then beneath the hem of her skirt, gradually making his way up to the curve of her ass. "Take off your top and bra so I can see your pretty breasts," he ordered.

She quickly drew the blouse over her head, then

unclipped her lacy bra, and the two garments joined the growing collection of clothes on the ground. He couldn't contain his deep groan of appreciation as her full, fuckable breasts bounced in front of him. His cock twitched with renewed lust as he ate her up with his eyes, his gaze coming to rest on her face.

Standing in front of him nearly naked, her hair now slightly disheveled, she was stunning and utterly magnificent, her skin pale and smooth like fresh cream. Her rosy areolas and pink, pouty nipples were a vivid contrast against all that luminous skin. Not sucking one of those hard peaks into his mouth was one of the most difficult things he'd ever forced on himself.

She reached behind her to unzip her short skirt, but he stopped her before she could execute the move. "Leave it," he said, and when she looked at him in confusion, he grinned up at her wickedly. "I want to fuck you with the skirt on."

With her breasts exposed and that tiny skirt covering her bare pussy beneath, she was *his* erotic fantasy come to life, as well as the bad girl *she* wanted to be.

Still sitting in his chair, he tipped his head as he stared into her hazy eyes and decided to ramp up the pleasurable stakes between them. "How dirty do you want this first time to be, Cupcake?"

"*So* dirty," she whispered, her features etched with sexual need as she pushed her fingers through his short hair. "Defile me, Clay. Make me yours, any way you desire."

*Jesus*, he thought, as his breath left his lungs in a rush. She'd just given him carte blanche with her body, and he planned to *defile* her in the most enjoyable, satisfying way.

He leaned back in his seat. "Straddle me, your legs on either side of my thighs," he instructed.

She moved in, her legs spread wide on either side of his. When she started to lower her ass to rest on his thighs, he grabbed her hips and pulled her back up. "No sitting," he ordered. "Put your hands on the chair by my head and brace yourself."

She did as he asked, the position automatically arching her upper body and placing her swaying breasts right in front of his face, right where he wanted them. He grinned up at her as he slipped a hand beneath her skirt and brushed his fingers up her inner thigh once again, her damp arousal greeting him even before he touched her weeping flesh.

"Keep your legs wide open. I want to finger fuck you," he said, as he dragged those same fingers between her soft folds and pushed two deep inside of her tight heat. "This way you can grind against my hand while I suck your gorgeous tits."

She whimpered and arched her back, offering up what he was dying to taste. He captured a nipple between his lips, flicked his tongue against the hard nub, and tugged it between his teeth before opening his mouth and taking as much of her as deep as he could. At the same time, he swept his thumb across her swollen clit and dragged his slickened fingers in and out of her, again and again, working her over until her sexy little body started to tremble and tense.

She tossed her head back, her uninhibited, panting breaths filling his ears. "Oh, God, oh, God, oh, God," she moaned wildly, as she shamelessly undulated her hips against the hand between her legs, brazenly seeking the release he could feel was right on the verge of splintering through her.

He scraped his teeth across a tender nipple and bit down on the taut bead of flesh, imparting just enough pain to send her over that final edge. She gasped for breath, her entire body jolting and shuddering as her internal muscles clenched around his stroking fingers.

She came on a soft cry of pleasure, a sound that went straight to his dick and made him ache for her all over again as a single thought haunted him.

*Would he ever get enough of her?*

# Chapter Eight

S AMANTHA COLLAPSED AGAINST Clay's chest, her
mind spinning in the aftermath of her phenomenal orgasm, his breathing just as erratic as her own.
Her face was tucked against his neck, and she'd
inadvertently trapped his arm between them—so his
long, thick fingers were still buried deep inside her
core, and her internal muscles clenched around him.

His arm twitched as he tried to remove his hand
from between her legs, but she was obviously dead
weight, and he couldn't budge.

"You need to sit back, Samantha," he said, his
voice a combination of amusement and gruff, aroused
man.

She leaned back on his thighs, surprisingly immod-
est about the fact that she was half naked and Clay was
staring hungrily at the breasts he'd just sucked on. She
shivered as he slid his fingers out of her, and groaned

softly as he purposely dragged the tips through her sensitive flesh.

As he held her gaze, he lifted his hand to his mouth and boldly licked and sucked her essence off his fingers. His eyes were hot and hungry like a wolf, and she knew that primal craving had nothing to do with food and everything to do with *her*.

"I want more," he said, and it wasn't a request but a demand.

Her body responded to that dark voice as if he had a direct connection to her sex. Clay, all alpha and dominant, obviously did it for her in a major way. *Who knew she liked being bossed around?* she mused.

She swallowed hard, because she wasn't sure what, exactly, he was referring to. "More?"

He curled a hand around the nape of her neck, guided her head toward him, and she went oh-so-willingly. *She was so easy when it came to him.* At first, she thought he was going to kiss her, but those sinful lips bypassed hers and settled against her ear instead.

"I want to eat you out and fuck you with my tongue," her murmured huskily.

A strangled sound caught in her throat, cutting off her ability to respond, and she felt her face heat in shock—even as a secret thrill spiraled through her.

He pulled back, saw the bright pink flush on her cheeks, and smirked. "You're the one who wanted it *so dirty*, Cupcake, so don't go all shy on me now," he said in a soft, mocking tone.

"I just didn't expect you to say something so…"

"Filthy?" he offered up as another devilish grin curved his full lips. "Consider it all part of me defiling you. Now sit up on the desk and spread your legs, unless you've changed your mind?"

She knew he was giving her an out, but her body was already humming in anticipation. She moved off his lap and perched her bottom on the edge of his desk. As he'd ordered, she opened her legs wide, but she instinctively smoothed the hem of her skirt down and over her thighs. Which was ridiculous considering what he'd just done to her. But it had been a long time since a man had been that up close and personal with her girly parts, and neither was she used to flaunting herself.

His thick, dark lashes fell half-mast as he moved his leather chair much, much closer. "You look so fucking hot with your breasts on display, yet so prim and proper with your hands in your lap and your skirt covering you so demurely."

He placed his palms on her knees and widened her legs even more. "Pull it up to your waist so I can see your bare pussy."

Another command she was compelled to obey. She gradually drew the material up her thighs like a slow strip tease, her stomach tumbling as his *I'm going to eat you up* gaze dropped to the sacred place she was about to reveal. Biting her bottom lip and summoning a heavy dose of confidence, she finally gathered the hem around her waist.

His breathing deepened, and he licked his lips

greedily as he stared at her sex. *"Fuck,"* he muttered, and pushed her hands out of the way. "Lean back so you can watch me as I *devour* you."

She braced her hands behind her so that her upper body was still angled in a way that gave her an unobstructed view. The chair he was sitting on was the perfect height, and she watched as he lowered his dark head and placed a hot, open-mouthed kiss on the inside of her thigh, his glittering eyes cast upward to lock with hers.

She shivered and moaned, and her sex pulsed with renewed desire as he lazily made his way upward, sucking, biting, and licking her skin until he arrived at his destination. He lifted her thighs so they draped over his shoulders and framed his strong jaw and face, and the erotic sight made her nearly come undone.

He slid his hands up over her hips and splayed them on her lower belly, then skimmed his thumbs downward to her pouty, glistening lips, so soft and wet from her first orgasm. He spread her open, exposing her clit to his heated gaze, and when he dipped his head and rubbed the light stubble on his jaw against that still-sensitive bud of flesh, she closed her eyes as wicked, forbidden desire nearly wrecked her. The stimulation was too much...yet not enough.

*"Watch me,"* he demanded, and as soon as her heavy-lidded gaze met his again, he dove right in and set out to obliterate everything she thought she knew about oral sex.

Nothing had prepared her for this devastation of

her senses, for being consumed and dominated and ravaged by a man who had no qualms about getting down and dirty. And messy. His open mouth was hot and hard on her, and she watched as his tongue slipped through her folds before spearing into her passage, so indecent and depraved and *she loved it.*

A soft cry broke free before she could catch it, and he relentlessly licked her again—a long, firm lap of his tongue that had her hips lifting to meet each teasing stroke that brought her precariously close to orgasm but stopped short of giving her what she so desperately needed.

"*Clay...*" she begged, her body on fire.

Another slow, torturous, swirling lick. "Is there something you want?" he muttered darkly, his breath so incredibly hot on her wet flesh.

He was going to make her ask for it, and she did. "I need to come. *Please.*"

Done playing with her, he latched on to her clit in earnest. His lips and tongue massaged the pleasure point with just the right amount of pressure and friction, and she reached down and twisted impatient fingers through his hair.

*More, more, more,* she silently chanted. Or maybe she said the words out loud, because he was sucking at her now, *eating at her,* and her head fell back as she rode his mouth and waves of the most sublime ecstasy shook her to the core, pleasure that never seemed to end. Until finally, the last tremor rumbled through her.

The one arm that was holding her up collapsed,

and she lay back on the desk, her legs falling over the sides. She was vaguely aware of Clay frantically searching the desk drawers.

"Is everything okay?" she asked, her body still tingling.

"No, I fucking need to get inside of you. *Now*." Another drawer slammed shut, and he opened another and riffled through the contents. "Mason left some condoms in here when he used my office for one of his sordid affairs a few weeks ago, and I tossed them into one of these drawers."

She laughed softly. "Your brother really is a manwhore, isn't he?"

"You have no idea," he muttered, then let out a triumphant *yes* when he found what he was looking for.

He tore the foil packet open with his teeth, and as she watched, he sheathed his huge, impressive cock that was raring to go again.

"I never would have thought that my brother's exploits would end up benefiting me," he said with a shake of his head.

Samantha had to admit, she was grateful to Mason, too, because she was dying to know what it felt like to be taken by this man who hadn't just taken over her body, he'd also possessed her soul. Nothing...absolutely *nothing* would ever be the same after this tryst. That much she knew with certainty.

She expected them to have sex face-to-face, so she was taken off guard when he pulled her off the desktop, spun her around, and bent her over, so that her arms were once again braced on the surface of the desk. He crowded up against her from behind, and her heart thumped hard in her chest, as she didn't know exactly what to expect.

He trailed his thumb down the center of her up-turned ass, stopping just before he reached the damp juncture of her thighs. "Spread your legs," he ordered gruffly.

*Oh, God.* She swallowed hard and did as she was told, bracing her feet apart and feeling a rush of cool air drift between her thighs. He'd warned her that he wasn't a traditional kind of guy when it came to sex, and had promised to *bend her over a table, spread her legs wide, and fuck her.* She'd even told him that she *wanted* that.

But she'd never anticipated feeling so vulnerable right before it happened.

"Do you still want this?" he asked softly from behind her, as if he'd just been intimately inside her mind.

The fact that he'd sensed her unease, that he was willing to stop if she just said the word, made her feel safe and secure with him. *She trusted him.* With her body. Her pleasure. With more? Heaven knew she wanted to. She was opening herself up to him, letting him in to places that no other man had ever touched before, but he'd warned her away, and she'd do well to respect that request, too.

But that didn't mean she'd call a halt. "Yes, I still

want this." She whispered the truth that she instinctively knew had the power to break her one day.

He exhaled a stream of breath, as if he'd been holding it while waiting for her answer. As if her *wanting this* meant more to him than just the hot sex he was offering.

Before she could over-think things even further, he placed his hands on her hips, slid his shaft between her legs, and pushed the head of his cock just a few inches inside her. She whimpered at the initial nudge. It wasn't nearly enough, and she instinctively pushed her ass back against him, seeking the hot slide of thick flesh filling her up. She needed it. Craved it. *Craved him.*

She rocked against him again, and he groaned, his fingers biting into her skin as he held himself back, restraining himself when his control was the last thing she wanted. She longed for heated passion and an irrational loss of control. She needed to know what it was like to really be *taken* by a man. *No, by Clay.*

"Do it," she urged him, then said the words she'd never spoken to another man before. "Fuck me, Clay. Now."

"*Christ,*" he growled, the need vibrating through him palpable. "This is going to be a hard, fast ride, Cupcake."

In the next instant, he shoved impossibly deep inside of her, wringing a shocked cry from her throat as her body attempted to adjust to the sudden and overwhelming invasion, along with the sensation of feeling so full. Fuller than she'd ever been before. He didn't give her time to catch her breath before he starting pumping into her, hard and relentless, with an urgency that seemed to increase with each driving thrust. His strong fingers bit into her waist, pulling her back again and again to meet every one of his rough, pounding strokes.

The way he dominated her was raw and gritty. But then again, so was *everything* about Clay. And somehow, despite all their inherent differences, it made her want him more, not less.

She moaned, lust overtaking her as she arched her back and shamelessly lifted her hips higher. The different angle of her body caused his shaft to rub against a sensitive patch of skin inside her, and stars flashed behind her eyes. Oh, God. That was so incredibly breathtaking, so deliciously good, and the ache between her legs coiled tighter and tighter, her climax just out of reach.

With every piercing, grinding thrust, he demanded her surrender, and Lord help her, she knew she'd willingly give it to him, along with anything else he wanted. *She was his.*

"Oh, God, *Clay*," she rasped, her orgasm gathering force inside her.

"*Give it to me*, Samantha. *Now*," he demanded, his voice dark and intense as he slid a hand between her legs and rubbed her clit, then tugged and pinched the throbbing, needy flesh between two fingers. "I want to feel you come on my cock."

His power and assertive demands were intoxicating, and she screamed as her release slammed through her in a rippling flood of sensation so potent and devastating it was like an out-of-body experience. Every muscle within her spasmed uncontrollably, gripping his cock in tight, clenching strokes as he continued to chase his own pleasure. Her climax was so raw and real, so stunning in its intensity, she didn't know how to handle it.

He wasn't far behind. A deep, possessive growl rumbled in his chest as he rammed into her frantically, pinning her so hard against the edge of the desk she suspected she'd have bruises tomorrow, *and she didn't care*. He swore, his hips jerking violently against her ass as he buried himself one last time, so deep inside her she didn't know where he ended and she began.

He left no part of her untouched. Physically, he owned her. Emotionally, he felt so right, so much a part of her. So inevitable. Like she'd been waiting her whole entire life to meet him, to be with him. She'd never had that kind of intimate and profound connection with a man before...and she feared she never would again.

# Chapter Nine

THURSDAY NIGHT WAS buy-one-get-one-free night for shots at Kincaid's, which always drew the younger crowd. A lot of the customers who came in on Monday for ladies' night returned to take advantage of yet another drink special and troll for a midweek hookup—and that included Mason, who was currently out on the dance floor getting down and dirty with the girl he'd been flirting with for the past hour.

Clay shook his head, knowing his brother would be in the woman's pants before the night was over, and as long as Mason didn't utilize the bathroom to screw his latest conquest, Clay would look the other way and not kick him out of the bar. But if Mason dared to use Clay's office, he'd castrate his sibling, because he didn't want anything tainting the memories of everything he'd done to Samantha in that room, and all the erotic ways he'd made use of his desk and made her his. Even if it had just been for that brief bit of time together.

Remembering how well Samantha had responded to him, how tight and hot she'd been around his cock, had his gaze searching for the woman who'd blown his mind, and his dick, just a few hours ago. Being with her had been sexy and dirty and so incredibly addicting he'd be a Goddamn liar if he said he wouldn't touch her again. Not now that he knew what her pussy tasted like and what her mouth felt like wrapped around his shaft. She'd left him reeling from the most earth-shattering encounter he'd ever had, and for the first time ever, he couldn't stop thinking about a woman long after sex was over.

*Yeah, he was so damned screwed.*

Clay stood at the far end of the bar, his gaze coming to rest on the object of his search. While Tara and Gina worked the service area, Samantha wove around the crowded tables, delivering drinks and food and taking orders. She was completely relaxed and glowing, no doubt from the three orgasms he'd given her earlier. The uncivilized caveman side of him took pride in the shine radiating from her porcelain skin and those luminous blue eyes.

She smiled at customers and laughed at something one of them said to her. The guy followed up his comment with a wink—which made Clay clench his jaw in irritation. Watching other men flirt and hit on Samantha was the worst part of her working at the bar. He didn't like seeing it happen nightly any more than he appreciated the fact that he *felt* that way about her at all.

Clay had never been a jealous, possessive kind of guy, and he had no business feeling that way now. He didn't do messy or complicated relationships with women, and he reminded himself that Samantha was no different. What they had was a short-term fling. He was too fucked up from his shitty past, too jaded by life in general, and too used to being alone to think otherwise. And mostly, he was too emotionally damaged to give any woman—Samantha, especially—the kind of love and forever promises she deserved and no doubt wanted.

He just didn't have it in him, and knowing that truth about himself had always enabled Clay to keep women compartmentalized in a way that ensured there were no misunderstandings, no unrealistic expectations. Just hot, uncomplicated sex. He attempted to keep Samantha in that same neat, temporary box in his brain—because he knew her time here was brief and merely a reprieve from her real life. It wouldn't be long before she either figured out what she wanted to do with her future and moved on or succumbed to parental pressure and returned home to marry the gutless bastard her father had chosen for her.

Clay's stomach twisted with real fucking pain at the notion, something he preferred not to think about now—or ever—even though he realistically knew that he'd never fit into her world. Socially, they were polar opposites. One way or another, her leaving was inevitable, and there was no way he'd try and stop her when the day arrived. In fact, he'd be doing her a huge favor by waving good-bye when the time came.

*Yeah, keep telling yourself that.* Whatever worked to let her go. As long as she didn't resort to option number two and choose home, along with the asshole waiting to put a ring on her finger. In the meantime, he'd do all he could to keep her happy while she was here—another anomaly for him, but fuck it. He wanted her happy, and that included encouraging her to pursue her interest in being a pastry chef.

Clay had given a lot of thought to the ways he could help Samantha in that regard. She didn't have a resume or the hands-on experience to impress a potential employer, but she *was* a certified pastry chef, and thanks to the housekeeper who'd initially taught her, she had honed her skills over the years. Her best bet was to find someone who'd let her prove her value and expertise in a less traditional way. It was an idea Clay was working on, and with Katrina's help, he had a surprise for Samantha he hoped would be ready tomorrow.

Out of the corner of his eye, Clay saw a guy sit a few barstools down from where he was standing. Reluctantly dragging his gaze away from Samantha, he turned toward the customer, only to realize that it was his youngest brother, Levi, who hadn't been in all week, which was fairly normal for Levi since he wasn't into the bar scene. So the fact that he was here now, on a very crowded night, told Clay that he'd stopped by for a specific purpose. And it wasn't difficult to figure out what that reason was, or whose big, fat mouth had gossiped like a fucking girl to their brother.

Tamping down his annoyance, he strolled over to where Levi was sitting. His twenty-four-year-old brother was the fairest of the three of them, with light green eyes and sandy blond hair. Clay had always assumed Levi had taken after whoever had fathered him, since he had none of their mother's features like he and Mason did.

"I take it you've talked to Mason?" Clay asked by way of a greeting.

"Not personally, though he did text me to tell me that you have a woman living with you," Levi replied with a raised brow. "You'd think big news like that would come directly from you, instead."

"She's not living with me in the way you mean," Clay explained, trying not to sound defensive.

"Doesn't matter *why* she's living with you," his brother said, his tone and gaze serious. "The fact that you *let* a woman stay in your apartment for more than a night is quite shocking and fascinating." Levi narrowed his gaze, studying Clay in that pensive way of his.

Even as a young boy, Levi had been the quiet one, always contemplating and analyzing a situation, and Clay had no doubt he was doing so now. Being a cop only amplified that personality trait, and Clay didn't like all that knowing speculation directed at him.

Glancing away, Clay grabbed a glass and filled it

CARLY PHILLIPS & ERIKA WILDE

with ice to make Levi's drink of choice—orange juice and soda water. Yeah, his brother was a teetotaler. After witnessing the harsh effects that alcohol and drugs had on a person's disposition as a kid, he'd never touched the stuff, unlike Mason, whose personality ran toward more destructive traits. Their middle brother got high however he could to forget the past and numb the pain.

"Samantha didn't have anywhere else to go since her family cut her off financially," Clay said, turning his thoughts back to Samantha as he poured the juice and soda water into the glass at the same time so they mixed together. "I'm just helping her get back on her feet."

"That's very charitable of you," Levi drawled as his gaze scanned the crowded bar area, then came back to Clay. "I take it she's the gorgeous blonde over there?"

Samantha was hard to miss, and she was the only waitress who Levi hadn't seen before. "Yeah, that's her." Clay set the orange juice spritzer on a napkin in front of his brother. "Her name is Samantha."

"Also known as Cupcake?" Levi tried covering the smirk on his lips by lifting his glass for a drink, but Clay caught the sly gleam in his eyes.

Clay glared at his brother. "Fuck Mason and his big mouth." And for being such an asshole, he thought grumpily.

Levi chuckled in amusement. "Ahh, brotherly love at its finest. Did you really expect anything less of Mason?"

Not trusting himself to reply to that comment with his own feelings about *brotherly love*, Clay instead grunted in response just as he saw Samantha come up to the service area to pick up a drink order. She looked over at him, her smile so sweet, sexy, and intimate he had no fucking idea what to do with the strange and unfamiliar emotions tightening his chest.

So he pushed the feelings away and lifted his hand to motion Samantha over. Her entire face lit up at his summons as she walked toward him.

"Hey, handsome," she flirted. "What can I do for you?"

Oh, hell, there were all kinds of suggestive innuendos in that question, and if they'd been alone, he would have played along, tossing out a dirty and descriptive response of what, exactly, she could do for him. Unfortunately, introductions were in order, and that speculative gleam was back in Levi's gaze as he watched the interaction between him and Samantha with too much interest.

With a groan, Clay said, "Samantha, I'd like you to meet my younger brother, Levi," he said, tilting his head toward the man she was standing next to. "He's a cop with Chicago PD."

Instead of the embarrassment Clay had expected, her grin widened, and her eyes shone with genuine pleasure as she turned toward his brother. "It's so great to meet you." She eagerly shook the hand that Levi offered.

"Likewise," Levi said with a smile.

Clay was suddenly grateful that his youngest sibling had better manners than Mason. At least around Samantha. Once she walked away, Clay was pretty sure the interrogation would ensue, and Levi was damn good at extracting information.

"So, you're the respectable brother," Samantha said, her tone light and humorous.

Levi raised a brow in surprise. "Excuse me?"

"Katrina," Clay said, knowing that was all the explanation his brother needed. The other woman had distinct opinions about each of the brothers' personalities, and they were pretty much on point.

"Ahhh," Levi said in understanding, then shrugged. "I suppose I am the respectable one, at least compared to Mason," he replied with a laugh.

"That's an understatement," Clay muttered. "There's a reason Katrina calls him a manwhore."

Samantha tipped her head, her blue eyes clear and way too guileless. "I just think Mason hasn't met the right woman yet."

Levi rolled his eyes at Clay, who let out a laugh.

"That's an optimistic thought, even for Mason," he said.

Levi nodded. "The man's got a point."

They both knew their middle brother much too well. He'd never had a relationship with a woman that was anything more than a few days, a week tops, of pure unadulterated sex. Not to mention, the *right woman* was right under his brother's nose, but Mason was either completely oblivious to her feelings or he didn't want to take a chance on Katrina and risk ruining the close bond and friendship they'd shared for so many years.

"Samantha, your order is up," Gina called from the service bar.

"I need to get back to work," Samantha said, though she smiled at Levi one last time. "I'm sure I'll see you around."

Levi watched her walk away, and as soon as she was out of earshot, he glanced back at Clay, that intuitive look back in his light green eyes. "This one is different, isn't she?"

Clay struggled to keep the truth locked away, because an affirmative answer would force him to evaluate those feelings that were stirring to life inside of him. Feelings that would acknowledge that *yes*, Samantha was different from any woman he'd been with before. She was unique and special—and so out of his league he was stupid to ever think otherwise.

"Whatever there may or may not be between us, it's casual, and only until she figures out what she wants to do next." He refused to give Levi any details about their relationship or admit just how in over his head he actually was.

Levi absently swirled the orange liquid in his glass, his gaze shrewd in a way that twisted Clay's insides. His brother was smart. Professionally and personally, he was observant, direct, and insistent. He also didn't beat around the bush and wouldn't be afraid to bring up shit Clay preferred to keep dead and buried.

If Clay was lucky, Levi would keep things focused on Samantha only. "What? Spit it out already," Clay muttered.

Levi placed his glass on the table, leaned forward, and met Clay's gaze. "If you honestly believe *this* woman is a casual fuck, then you're a goddamn idiot."

Clay bristled. "I know what I'm doing."

Levi released an insipid laugh and shook his head. "You don't know shit. I saw the intimate way she looked at you," he said as he folded his arms on the surface of the bar. "And more importantly, before you saw me, I noticed the way *you* looked at *her*. Like you were ready to vault over the counter if any guy in the place so much as laid a hand on her. I've never seen such a possessive look in your eyes. *That's* how I know Samantha is different."

Clay clenched his jaw, hating that he'd been so transparent. "I barely know Samantha." The lie burned in his throat.

"I know our mother didn't give us a reason to trust women," Levi said, diving right into that forbidden territory Clay had hoped to avoid. "She didn't give a shit about us, and Wyatt was even worse," his brother went on, daring to bring up the mean son of a bitch their mother had left them with. The bastard who'd had no qualms about beating the crap out of them on a regular basis.

"Shut up," Clay said through clenched teeth. He didn't talk about Wyatt, *ever*.

Levi narrowed his gaze. "How long are you going

to let what our mother and Wyatt did to us dictate your future and happiness?" he asked, ignoring Clay's warning to end this discussion now.

Nausea swirled in his stomach as the grim memories he preferred to keep buried threatened to strangle him. A rising anger followed, but his brother was on a fucking roll, and now that he'd pried open Pandora's box and let out all the ugliness of their past, there was no stopping him.

"No one's perfect. Hell, everyone has a past that has shaped who they are. And no matter what you think or feel about what Wyatt did to you, you are a good person, Clay."

Clay gripped the towel on the bar and shut his eyes tight. There was nothing he could do to forget Wyatt's abuse or the single night that had changed Clay from a boy to a man intent on killing another human being. He'd had so much rage coursing through his veins and no hesitation about stabbing the knife he'd stolen to protect his brothers straight into Wyatt's dark, evil heart. Unfortunately, despite all the bloodshed, the mean bastard had lived.

"Stop stirring up shit," Clay said in a low, menacing voice he barely recognized as his own.

"Is that what I'm doing?" Levi asked, unfazed by Clay's anger. "If you'd just talk about it instead of pretending it never happened, then maybe you'd quit hiding behind this bar and meaningless women." Levi eyed him knowingly. "Better yet, maybe you won't let the one worthwhile woman get away."

Clay braced his hands on the edge of the bar and sent his brother a dangerous look. "Let it fucking go, Levi," he said in his most threatening tone. "I don't need a lecture, and our shitty past has nothing to do with any kind of relationship I have with Samantha."

"No, it's just holding you back from having any kind of relationship at all." Levi sighed, the sound rife with frustration. "You don't always have to be so damn strong for everyone, Clay, and you don't have to carry the burden alone. If you remember, I was there, too."

"I fucking remember *everything*, Levi." How could he ever forget when the nightmares plagued him on a regular basis? It had been the worst night of his life, and that was saying something considering all the horrible things the three of them had endured as kids. He still had the physical scars to remind him every damn day what they'd gone through.

Clay exhaled a stream of breath that did nothing to ease the pressure in his chest. "Now that you're done psychoanalyzing me, feel free to leave, because I have work to do."

"Of course you do," Levi said sarcastically as he slid off the barstool, clearly knowing he was being dismissed. "Have a good night, Clay."

Was his brother seriously wishing him a *good night* after tangling his emotions into a giant fucking knot?

Clay glared at Levi and flipped him the middle finger, uncaring that anyone in the place might see the rude gesture. "Fuck you for screwing up my night, asshole."

"You're welcome." There wasn't an ounce of re-gret in Levi's eyes or expression. Mission obviously complete, Levi turned and strode out of the bar, leaving Clay alone with memories that were now raw and perilously close to the surface.

# Chapter Ten

SAMANTHA ATE BREAKFAST and washed the dishes, her mind preoccupied with Clay, who'd been gone before she'd woken up this morning. She'd thought what had happened in his office last night had been more than just sex, and she couldn't help but feel disappointed at being alone again.

She had truly thought that things had changed between them. That he'd quit trying to avoid her. But she'd noticed a distinct shift in Clay's mood after his brother Levi had left. He'd seemed angry about something, and even when she'd had a moment from her busy tables to ask him if everything was okay, he'd given her an abrupt "I'm fine" that had told her he was far from okay but whatever was bothering him wasn't up for discussion.

So, last night she'd given him space, even though she hated the distance he'd created between them.

After the bar had closed and she and the other employees were done with their light cleanup, she'd realized that Clay was in his office—with the door closed—which was equivalent to a loud *stay away from me* sign posted on the frame. Tara confirmed that she'd heard Clay and Levi arguing, and while Samantha wanted Clay to know he could talk to her if he needed a listening, non-judgmental ear, she instinctively knew that he wasn't the kind of man to discuss personal issues or one to dissect his feelings with a woman. No, Clay was controlled and guarded, emotionally and physically. He was always there for other people and his employees, listening and caring about their problems, but in the short time Samantha had known him, it was apparent that Clay wasn't comfortable when it came to opening up to others, and especially her.

It was incredibly frustrating, considering she wanted to know so much more about Clay Kincaid. He'd given her little tidbits of his past, just enough for her to know his childhood hadn't been ideal. Unfortunately, he was excellent at deflecting any attempt she made to dig a little deeper in hopes of learning what experiences had molded him into the man he was today— one who was generous and reliable and decent, yet so emotionally guarded.

Last night, she'd come upstairs and had taken a shower, intending to wait up until Clay finally came up to the apartment. But the moment her tired body had sunk into his soft mattress and her head had hit the pillow, she'd been out. And by the time she'd gotten up this morning, he was already gone.

It felt as though they were back to square one, and Samantha refused to let Clay retreat from them, *from her*, after finally making progress with him yesterday afternoon.

She'd just finished drying the last dish when someone knocked on the door that led out of the apartment to the side lot, where deliveries to the bar were made, and where the employees parked their vehicles. She figured whoever was there, it had to be for Clay, but since he wasn't around, she headed for the door.

She looked through the peephole and saw Katrina standing on the other side. Samantha unlocked and opened the door, happy to see someone she already considered a friend.

"Hey, what are you doing here?" Samantha asked curiously, her gaze taking in the other woman's outfit. She experienced a moment of envy at the way Katrina could pull off wearing a dark brown suede top that laced together in the front and made her look tough and sexy at the same time. The tight fit pushed up her breasts and made them look amazing. She had on a matching miniskirt and cute beige suede ankle boots with a nice-sized heel.

"I have a delivery for you," Katrina said, flashing a smile.

"Me?" Samantha laughed, now even more confused. "I don't remember ordering anything."

"You didn't. Clay did." Katrina shook her head and waved her hand in the air, making those colorful butterflies inked on her arm appear as if they were taking flight. "Or rather, Clay told me what he wanted to do, and I did the ordering because there is no way he could have pulled this off on his own," she said, looking very pleased with herself.

Samantha had absolutely no idea what Katrina was talking about, but she was definitely intrigued. She followed the other woman's pointing gesture down to the parking lot, where two young, muscular men stood next to a small, nondescript delivery truck, waiting.

"Bring it all up here, boys!" Katrina called out.

For the next fifteen minutes, Samantha stood in the living room with Katrina while the guys brought up delivery after delivery of boxes and large-handled bags from Williams-Sonoma—a high-end store that sold the best of kitchen equipment and small appliances, professional bakeware, and specialty items. She was so stunned she was speechless. When one of the men carried in a big box with a picture of an industrial-grade stand mixer on the side, Samantha's jaw nearly dropped to the floor as understanding finally dawned.

"Oh, my God," she breathed, both shocked and elated by what Clay had done. He'd taken her dream of being a pastry chef and was helping to make it a reality.

"He bought all this stuff for me to use to bake, didn't he?" she asked incredulously.

"Yep," Katrina confirmed. "I wasn't sure what, exactly, you would need, so I asked a consultant at the store to put together everything a new pastry chef would need to have in her kitchen, including all the ingredients you might need to do the baking," she said, sounding as excited as Samantha felt. "You should be well equipped since I pretty much cleared out the baking aisle at the grocery store."

By the time the delivery guys had unloaded everything, the entire kitchen was filled with bags and boxes, and Samantha couldn't help but feel overwhelmed on a multitude of levels. "It's too much." She pressed her hands to her warm cheeks when she thought about how much Clay had spent on her. A surge of guilt wasn't far behind. "All this had to have cost him a small fortune."

"Meh," Katrina said with a shrug, as if money wasn't an issue. "Clay didn't hesitate when I told him how much everything was."

He truly hadn't spared any expense on her aspirations, and even without words, he was letting her know that he believed in her, when her parents never had and never would. He had no idea how much his generosity meant to her, or how much his confidence in her abilities boosted her own determination to make her dreams a reality. She didn't want to let herself down, but more importantly, she didn't want to let *him* down.

An emotional lump formed in Samantha's throat, and tears pricked the backs of her eyes. All her life, she'd received ridiculously expensive presents—opulent jewelry, extravagant cars and trips, luxurious designer clothes and accessories—but she'd never been given a gift that was so personal and heartfelt. So thoughtful and meaningful. Even with her parents knowing how much she loved to bake and how badly she wanted to pursue being a pastry chef, not once had they ever encouraged her, let alone given her something to acknowledge her passion.

In that moment, Samantha felt that first flutter of sensation in her heart that told her she was on her way to falling in love with Clay Kincaid. She ought to provide herself with a stern lecture about this thing with Clay being just an affair, a warning about guarding her heart or else she'd get hurt. But as she stared at the abundance of items beckoning to her in the fully stocked kitchen in *Clay's* apartment, she couldn't find the words, or the will to ignore the feelings growing inside her. And she no longer wanted to, she realized.

She glanced at Katrina, who'd been watching her reaction the entire time. "I need to go thank him."

Before she could head downstairs to the bar, Katrina placed a hand on her arm. "Tell you what. How about you start going through the bags and boxes to unpack and see everything you have, and *I'll* go and get Clay."

Like a little kid at Christmas, Samantha couldn't deny that she was dying to check out the goods. "Okay," she said, and the first thing she did was unpack the beautiful industrial-grade stand mixer in her favorite color—bright pink.

✧  ✧  ✧

KATRINA FOUND CLAY in the storeroom, where he was busy going through his liquor inventory. With an anxious sensation in his stomach, he watched her sashay toward him, her mischievous green eyes sparkling like emeralds.

Clay knew why Katrina was here. She'd texted him almost a half an hour ago to let him know that she'd arrived with the delivery truck and unloading was about to commence. Considering it had been his idea to supply Samantha with everything she needed to bake her desserts, he knew Katrina had expected him to be there when everything arrived.

He'd seriously thought about it, but he'd felt a little off this morning after last night's chat with Levi. Okay, that was an understatement. He'd been moody and angry and not at all happy that his brother had poked and prodded and brought up emotions he worked hard to keep buried. Levi had pissed him off, and his nasty mood was the last thing he wanted to subject Samantha to—or have to explain.

So when he'd woken up this morning still feeling on edge, he'd decided to head to the gym for a hard workout, which had helped burn off some steam. He'd showered and changed at the fitness center, and by the time he'd returned to the bar, his annoyance toward his brother had abated, but then he'd realized that he was suddenly unsure of his impulsive decision to buy what amounted to a pastry kitchen for Samantha. He was worried about her reaction to his gifts. What if she thought it was stupid? What if she didn't appreciate him butting into her business? What if she took the gesture for more than what it was, especially after yesterday afternoon?

And when the fuck had he become so concerned about making a woman happy?

Katrina crossed her arms over her chest and pinned him with a discerning look. "I texted you half an hour ago. I expected you to come upstairs and see what your thousands of dollars bought for Samantha."

He shrugged casually and set his clipboard on a shelf. "I got distracted with inventory."

She had the grace not to call him out on his lie. Instead, she smiled and said, "I have to say, you certainly know the way to this woman's heart."

"She liked everything?" he asked, trying like hell not to sound like an infatuated teenager who wanted to impress the girl he was crushing on. Jesus, he was so pathetic.

Katrina rolled her eyes and shifted on her ridiculously high heels. "You're kidding me, right? I don't think I've ever seen a woman so thrilled to get kitchen appliances as a gift from a man. Most of us girls prefer diamonds or a pair of Louboutins, but I'm coming to realize that Samantha is unique."

Relieved by Katrina's reassurance, he laughed, and the sound finally released the tension he'd been carrying since his brother's visit. Yes, she *was* unique, considering the comfortable, wealthy, want-for-nothing life she'd walked away from, and that was one of the things he found so attractive about her. She was so unassuming, so gracious. *So unique.*

"I had fun surprising Samantha, but I need to get back to Inked before your brother starts blowing up my phone with texts demanding to know where I am," Katrina said with a put-out sigh. "I didn't tell him I was running errands for you."

"You didn't?" he asked, surprised to hear that. "Why not?"

Her chin jutted out stubbornly. "Because it's none of his fucking business, and I'm done being at his beck and call."

Katrina's defiant attitude had Clay biting back a smile. As the manager of Inked, Katrina had been putting up with Mason's bullshit for a few years now, but it appeared she was finally fed up with his brother taking advantage of her and their friendship. He had a feeling that Mason had no clue that there was a brewing storm heading his way.

Not wanting to get into the middle of that skirmish, he changed the subject. "Thanks for everything," he said, sincerely grateful for her assistance since he didn't know jack about baking. "I couldn't have pulled this off without your help."

"It was my pleasure. I'm going to head out, but Samantha is waiting for you upstairs, so go and enjoy her excitement." Katrina walked toward the storeroom door but turned around before exiting and met his gaze. "And just for the record, I really like her. A lot."

"I do, too," he replied automatically. *Way too much.*

Once Katrina was gone, Clay made his way up to

the apartment and quietly slipped inside. Samantha was in the kitchen, and there was so much stuff on the counters that it boggled his mind. Currently, she was testing out a mixer in a bright pink color that suited her personality. She turned it on, and as an electronic whirring sound filled the space, she bounced on the balls of her bare feet enthusiastically and let out a giddy laugh that made him grin.

He took a moment to just watch her as she *ooh*ed and *aah*ed over different bakeware and appliances that seemed to impress her. Her hair was in a ponytail, and she was wearing a white tank top and a pair of faded jean shorts that molded to that perfect ass he'd had the enjoyment of caressing yesterday afternoon while taking her from behind. The hot memory made his cock twitch—*no shock there*—and he redirected his dirty thoughts before they escalated even further. As much as he wanted Samantha, this moment was about her and not his unruly dick.

He leaned against the nearby wall, shoved the tips of his fingers into his jean pockets, and cleared his throat, making his presence known. "Does everything meet with your approval?" he asked.

She spun around, her eyes wide with elation. Her undisguised gratitude was like a warm ray of sunshine on his soul, and the happiness etching her beautiful features made every penny he'd spent well worth her delighted reaction. And when she looked at him as if he'd given her the moon and stars, he wanted to give her more. Hell, he wanted to give her *everything*.

"I can't believe you did all this," she said, her voice filled with wonder and a wealth of appreciation.

He shrugged, trying to remain nonchalant. "If you want to be a pastry chef, then you need to bake. I just supplied you with the means to make that happen." But they both knew the gesture was much more than that.

She closed the distance between them, stopping so close that he could see the affection for him in her eyes, along with a tenderness that nearly slayed him. *Nobody* had ever looked at him that way before.

"Thank you, Clay," she said, her voice thick with an emotion that made his heart beat hard and fast in his chest. "I can't tell you how much this means to me."

She wrapped her arms around his neck and hugged him, and something inside of him cracked open and shifted. As a kid, he'd grown up without physical affection, had never been hugged by his own mother. As an adult, he didn't cuddle with women and avoided any kind of lingering embrace because it felt awkward to him. But this...the feel of Samantha's body pressing against him was so intimate, the connection between them so honest and real...and he liked it.

And it had nothing to do with sex. Forcing his stiff body to relax, he tentatively circled his arms around her waist, pulling her closer and holding her tight against him. She was so soft and warm, and he closed his eyes, inhaling the scent of her skin and savoring the moment that was very much a first for him.

She pulled back, and he reluctantly let her go, though she only took a single step back. Her hands slid down to his chest, and she kept them there, her face tipped up to his.

"I will pay you back for everything," she promised, suddenly much too serious. "Every single cent. I swear it."

"It's a gift, Cupcake," he said, and gave in to the urge to run the back of his fingers along the smooth, soft skin of her cheek. "You don't repay something that is given to you."

"I can't just take all of this." She shook her head. "The money—"

"Isn't an issue," he said, cutting her off. And it truly wasn't, but he could see the doubts in her eyes, so he tried for a compromise of sorts. "Tell you what, how about you repay me by baking your favorite dessert?"

Her eyes lit up at the suggestion, the excitement back on her face. "My favorite dessert isn't anything fancy or extravagant," she warned him. "Are you sure you don't want me to make you something fancier, like a chocolate profiterole or an éclair?"

He laughed. "Do I look like a guy who dines on fancy éclairs and whatever that other thing is called? I want *your* favorite dessert."

"Okay," she agreed, bouncing once again on her feet, as if she could barely contain her renewed enthusiasm. "Will you stay up here and keep me company?"

He couldn't refuse her. Didn't want to, anyway.

"Sure."

He sat down on one of the dining chairs facing the kitchen, content to watch Samantha in her element. Now that he'd given her something specific to do, she was focused on creating. She went through the bags, pulling out more items she needed and setting them on the counter, and even went to the refrigerator to retrieve a fresh lemon. That was his only hint as to what she was making. With her back to him, he couldn't see what she was mixing together, all of which she was doing without a recipe and completely by memory.

Fifteen minutes later, he caught a glimpse of a tray going into the oven, and she continued to move about the kitchen, sorting through the grocery sacks for other items while keeping that pink mixer on and churning ingredients. She was so intent on her work that he didn't disturb her with conversation. It was enough for him to see how much she loved baking, and he didn't want to break her concentration.

Xena came sauntering out of the bedroom and jumped onto his lap, and he turned his attention to the cat, who was rubbing against his chest and demanding her fair share of attention. He smoothed his hand along her spine, and she began to purr. He continued to pet her until she'd had enough and jumped back down to graze on the cat food in her bowl.

Before long, Samantha took the tray out of the oven, and the scent of something sweet and lemony permeated the air. She deliberately blocked his view of whatever else she was doing, so he pulled out his cell phone and checked to make sure he didn't have any important calls or messages. He answered a few emails and played a couple of games of Tetris, not realizing just how much time he'd killed until Samantha finally spoke.

"Okay, here it is. My very favorite dessert."

He shut down the game and glanced up as Samantha walked toward him holding a plate. He couldn't help but grin when he finally got a glimpse of what she'd been creating.

"A cupcake?" he asked incredulously, the irony of *that* not lost on him.

"Not just *any* cupcake," she assured him with a bit of sass as she came to a stop next to his chair. She lowered the dish so he could look at a very *fancy*-looking sweet treat. "This here is a lemon cupcake, with an *amazing* lemon cream curd inside and melt-in-your-mouth lemon buttercream frosting swirled on top. I can guarantee that this is the best thing you will ever put in your mouth."

He shook his head, treating her to a wicked-sounding chuckle as he cast his eyes up to hers. "Maybe the second, third, or fourth best thing," he corrected as he skimmed his fingers up the inside of her smooth thigh. "But definitely not *the* best thing I've ever tasted or put into my mouth," he said, pressing his fingertips against the seam of her jean shorts, his insinuation clear.

She sucked in a breath but did nothing to stop the

pressure and friction of his fingers rubbing slowly but firmly between her legs.

"You're so bad," she said, her husky voice matching the desire flaring bright in her blue eyes.

"I can be even naughtier," he assured her, his cock swelling in response to the sexy game they were playing, along with the way her nipples poked against the cotton tank top she was wearing, silently imploring him to lick and bite. "Would you like me to tell you what those other things are that taste as sweet as candy?"

"No." She licked her lips, her lashes falling half-mast. "I want you to eat my cupcake."

The small, playful smile canting the corners of her mouth told him that she'd chosen her words deliberately, in reference to the nickname he'd given her.

"I've already had a taste of the best cupcake I'm ever going to have," he assured her. "But if you sit on my lap, I'll try this lemon one."

"Thank you for indulging me," she teased, even though they both knew that, before they were done, he'd be sampling more than just her baked treat.

She set the plate on the table, and instead of sitting across his lap, she brazenly straddled his hips, her ass settled on his thighs. They were sitting face-to-face, the crotch of her shorts aligned with the stiff erection straining against the fly of his jeans. She rocked subtly against his aching dick, and he groaned deep in his throat, a hot surge of need twisting through him.

He grabbed her hips before she could do it again.

"You'd better feed me a bite of that cupcake before I change my mind and eat *you* instead," he said gruffly.

She shivered at his sexy threat, but she obviously *really* wanted him to try her dessert, because she behaved. Picking up the fork that was resting on the plate, she used the tines to cut out a portion of the confection so that he could taste everything at once—the cake, the filling, and the frosting—and fed him the sample.

As soon as the tart and sweet lemony flavors hit his taste buds, a moan of appreciation rose in his throat. By far, the cupcake was the best dessert he'd ever had, and he was impressed by her baking skills. The cake itself was moist, the filling like lemon silk, and the frosting *did* melt in his mouth.

The cupcake on the plate, decorated with frosting that looked like a delicate swirl of ribbons and lace, was as professional looking as...the one he'd seen looking through the bakery window in town when he'd been a young boy. The long-ago memory popped into his head.

"When I was a kid..." He blinked, hearing his voice and realizing what he'd been about to reveal. He stopped short, cutting off the words and the memory.

She tipped her head, looking at him curiously. "When you were a kid, what?" she prompted.

He shook his head. "Nothing."

"It was obviously something," she persisted. "What happened when you were a kid? Were you not allowed to have cupcakes?" she asked, her gaze holding his hostage.

It was a good guess on her part, based on what she knew about his childhood, which wasn't much. But it was obviously enough for her to come to that conclusion. He seriously thought about deflecting the conversation, but the soft, compassionate look in her eyes compelled him to share something he'd rather not even think about.

"When I was a kid, for the longest time I didn't know what cupcakes were," he said, not surprised to see her eyes widen in shock.

"How...how is that even possible?" She frowned in disbelief.

He exhaled a deep breath and finished what he'd started. "My brothers and I never had a birthday party, and the school I went to didn't allow outside food, not even on special occasions. We didn't have a TV, and we got our groceries from a local food bank that just provided the basics."

It was the most profound glimpse he'd given anyone into his past, and because it was Samantha, it felt good to share something so difficult, yet painful at the same time.

"Oh, Clay..." She placed her hands gently on either side of his face. That same tenderness he'd seen earlier was back in her gaze, this time laced with compassion, and it drew him in and tugged on emotions he usually kept locked down tight.

He swallowed hard and forced himself to continue. "The first time I saw cupcakes was when I was walking home from school. I was about seven years old, and I passed by this upscale bakery in town. I looked in the window and saw these little cakes that looked so good I couldn't stop staring. I was so hungry, and I wanted one so badly, but as soon as the woman inside saw me outside her shop, she came out and literally chased me away."

A flash of sadness followed by anger sparked in her eyes. "Why would she do that to a little boy?"

He knew exactly why, and since he'd already come this far, he answered her question honestly. "Because the people in town knew me as a low-life Kincaid. The bastard child of a crack whore. And having a poor, dirty kid standing outside of their store wasn't good for business."

She gave him a heartbroken look as her thumbs stroked along his jaw, her touch gentle and oddly comforting. "I'm so sorry," she whispered.

He shrugged, pretending it no longer mattered. "It was a long time ago."

She clearly wanted to say something more, but she smiled impishly at him instead, and he was grateful that she let it go.

"I will make you as many cupcakes as you like," she said, his heart melting a little at her sincere promise. "Anytime you want." And the serious mood that had settled between them dissipated in an instant.

He laughed, appreciating her lighthearted comment, and he let the past memories go in favor of more decadent, imminent pleasures. "*You* are the only cupcake I need," he told her as he promptly stripped off her tank top, then unhooked her bra and dropped it to the floor, baring her gorgeous breasts to his gaze, his hands, his mouth. "But I do think you need a little frosting."

His little vixen nodded eagerly. "Yes, I think so, too," she agreed as she shifted restlessly on his thighs, once again massaging his thickening cock against her denim-clad sex.

Grinning at how impatient she already was, he dipped his finger into the froth of lemon-flavored icing and dabbed a generous amount on both of her tight nipples. Her lips parted on a gasp, which then turned into a sweet, sweet moan of need when he pushed her full breasts up with his hands and set out to clean up the mess he'd made.

He flicked his tongue across each taut bead of flesh and used his teeth to scrape across those delectably perky nipples that tasted like spun sugar laced with a touch of lemon extract. *Yum.* He opened his mouth wider, taking her breast deeper while sucking and licking off the last bit of the tasty treat.

She exhaled on a soft moan of pleasure and slid her fingers through his hair. Her head fell back, and her spine arched for more of his mouth as she brazenly rode his stiff cock through their jeans, grinding against him in a mindless, lust-induced fog.

Heat, sharp and demanding, slammed through him. *Jesus Christ*, if she didn't stop her erotic lap dance, he was going to come in his jeans like a horny teenager who had no self-control. But that's what Samantha did to him. She stripped away all his restraint, made him wild and desperate to be so deep inside her she'd never forget he was there. That she was *his*.

No matter how unrealistic, that possessive thought drove him, along with the pounding, pulsing need to feel her body tighten around his cock and milk him dry. Until he realized he had no protection on him.

He pulled his mouth from her swollen nipple and swore, the sound harsh and frustrated. "I need to get a condom."

Shit, talk about a buzzkill, but there was no way he'd take any kind of risk with her.

She slowly lifted her lids, her heavy lashes shadowing her eyes, but there was no mistaking the beguiling smile curving her pink lips. "Actually, I have one in the front pocket of my shorts."

He blinked at her, surprised by her unexpected announcement. "You do?"

She giggled, the sound adorably playful and naughty as she pulled out a foil wrapper and gave it to him. "I found a box of condoms in your bathroom drawer, and I wanted to be prepared when this happened again."

He was both grateful and relieved at her foresight. The fact that she was so sure they'd have sex again that she'd kept a condom on her at all times so it wouldn't be an issue made him harder than he already was.

He guided her off his lap so that she was standing

in front of him. Looking up at her, he unsnapped her shorts, unzipped them, and let them drop to the ground. "You're such a naughty, dirty girl," he teased.

"With you, I am," she admitted, and to prove her point, without an ounce of modesty, she pushed her panties down her legs and kicked them off, too, leaving her completely naked to his gaze.

Goddamn, she was gorgeous. Her body so sleek yet curvy in all the right places. So sensual and sexy he knew he'd never get enough of her, no matter how many times he fucked her.

"Sit down on the table," he ordered as he pulled his T-shirt over his head, then nearly ripped open the front of his jeans so that he could sheathe his cock and be ready to drive into her. Just as soon as he sampled her dessert in one more place.

"Lean back and spread your legs, Cupcake," he demanded, dying to get a taste of her once again. "I haven't had my fill of this delicious frosting yet."

She did as he asked, parting her thighs wide and opening herself up to him completely. Her pussy was so plump and wet, and the glistening folds separated to reveal that pearl of flesh nestled at the hood of her sex. He raked his gaze up the length of her body until he reached her face. She was biting her lower lip, and the flush sweeping across her cheeks had nothing to do with being shy. No, the pink tinge, and the escalating rise and fall of her breasts, was pure anticipation.

He wasn't going to disappoint. He dragged his thumb through the frosting, then smeared the creamy substance across her clit and down her slit so he'd have every excuse to slide his tongue in every single crevice to clean it all up. When he reached the wettest part of her, her hips jerked against his hand and her breath hitched in her throat. Undeterred, he pushed two thick fingers all the way inside of her and used his thumb to swipe across her sticky clit once again.

"Clay…" Her voice rasped with burning, escalating need.

He understood that hunger, because it was pulsing through his veins and racing straight to his cock. Done waiting, done teasing, he bent down and buried his mouth between her thighs and devoured his cupcake. His swirling tongue lapped up all traces of the frosting as he pumped his fingers in and out of her passage, and when he sucked on her sensitive clit, she cried out and grabbed a handful of his hair—not to pull his mouth closer, but to yank his head away.

He looked up at her, not sure why she stopped him when he knew she'd been a few well-placed licks away from an orgasm.

"I need you inside of me, Clay," she said huskily. "Now. Please."

The demanding passion in her gaze—in her words—fueled his own lust, and he suddenly couldn't wait to get balls deep inside of her. He shoved his jeans a bit lower on his thighs so they were out of the way without him having to take the time to strip them off. "Get off the table and turn around." The order came out more forceful than he'd planned, but she had a way of bringing out the aggressive, more dominant edge in him.

She shook her head and remained right where she was, in the same spread-open position, too. "No."

"No?" He didn't know whether to grin at her impudence or turn her around so he could smack her ass for being insubordinate.

"No," she reiterated, then blew his fucking mind with her next brazen request. "I want you to take me like this. This time, I want to watch you..."

"Watch me do what?" he prompted, wanting to hear her say those filthy words.

She licked her bottom lip and gave him what he was waiting for. "I want to watch you fuck me," she said, her voice soft as a caress to his aching cock. "And I want to watch you as you come."

*Jesus,* he thought, and couldn't deny that he wanted to stare into those sultry blue eyes as she climaxed, too. He lined up the tip of his shaft against her slick entrance, then grabbed her hips to keep her securely in place as he drove into the softest, hottest, most addicting pussy he'd ever had.

He could feel her tight body clasp every inch of him as he pushed deeper, deeper. *Oh, fuck,* so deep he was completely and utterly lost in her. Physically, yes, but it was also the ferocious need he felt for this woman alone that made his pleasure so damn intense he shook with the restraint it took not to take her like a man possessed.

Her breath shuddered as he filled her up, and she

wrapped her legs around his waist, bracing him as he started to thrust in and out. He moved slowly enough that they were both able to watch her body swallow his thick shaft, then he withdrew until just the tip of his erection was inside of her, then pushed forward once again.

He took a moment to appreciate the sexy slope of her lush, full breasts and tight, suckable nipples—and the way her naked tits bounced every time he shoved back into her. She looked so fucking hot naked, and the whole visual aspect of their position made it all the more erotic.

It also sorely tested his self-control and made his hips instinctively rock faster and harder against her as his orgasm sizzled to the surface. At this rate, he knew he wasn't going to last long, and he wanted her with him when he climaxed.

"Touch yourself," he said gruffly, unable to move his hands from her hips. "I'm already so damn close. Make yourself come for me."

She didn't hesitate to put her fingers on her clit, another seductive visual that sent a surge of lust pulsing through him. Moaning softly, she circled and rubbed that taut nub of flesh, and his release beckoned like the devil.

"*Come*, Samantha," he growled as he kept up the maddening pace of his thrusts while trying desperately to stave off the searing heat gathering low in his belly and weakening his resolve. "*Now.*"

Her eyes glazed over with desire yet remained

steady on his face. "Not until you do first," she said huskily, as those slender fingers continued to stroke over her slick flesh. "I want to watch you."

An unbelievable gasp of laughter escaped him at her shameless challenge. She was fucking killing him, in the very best way, and if she wanted to see how wild she made him, then he wasn't going to hold back, trusting that she wouldn't be far behind him.

Breathing hard and clenching his jaw, Clay kept his eyes locked on hers as he pumped into her rhythmically, harder and faster, again and again, until the tight, red-hot friction clasping his cock was more than he could resist.

*Come on, come on, come on,* he silently chanted, no longer able to wait for her as his stomach muscles tensed and his release ripped through him. A harsh groan rumbled in his chest as he bucked uncontrollably against her, sensation after sensation battering him like a sledgehammer.

And just when he thought it couldn't get any more mind-blowing, her body shook with her own orgasm, and her inner walls gripped him insanely tight, rippling and squeezing every last ounce of pleasure out of his cock until he had nothing left to give.

# Chapter Eleven

THE NEXT TWO weeks became a regular routine of sex, desserts, and work. But mostly sex and desserts, Samantha thought with a grin as she arranged her just-finished French macarons on a plate. She'd spent every day baking something different, and she'd never been happier or more in her element. Without a doubt, she knew this was what she wanted to do with her life, and she was finally ready to take the next step to make this dream of hers happen.

Which also meant big changes between her and Clay. He just didn't know it yet.

She'd managed to repay him for the clothes and toiletries she'd bought in her first days here, and had saved most of her tip money and weekly pay since. After a lot of deliberation, she'd also pawned the Chopard diamond watch and Mikimoto pearl necklace she'd worn the night she'd come into the bar, and sent the claim ticket to her mother with no return address on the envelope. At least that way her parents had the choice of retrieving the items if they wanted them back. They'd purchased the jewelry for no special reason other than that her mother could afford it and wanted to make sure Samantha only wore the best that well-known designers had to offer. There had been no sentimental value attached to either piece, something that saddened her but made them much easier to part with for cash.

The high-end jewelry had given her a few extra thousand dollars, which she'd used to open a checking and savings account at a nearby bank. She'd purchased a cell phone in her own name, as well. She never again wanted to be in the helpless position of not having money of her own. She no longer wanted to depend on her parents for anything other than their love...something she wasn't sure they'd be willing to provide without strings. And was that really love?

She shook her head, knowing she might have to accept that her parents weren't capable of the honest, giving emotion. Something she'd deal with if and when the time came. For now, they'd left her alone, no doubt hoping she'd fail and come running back. Since that wouldn't be happening, she couldn't help but wonder what kind of reception she'd receive when she made the attempt to talk to either one of them again.

All she wanted was to be her own person and be able to make her own choices. To have the freedom to pursue the things that made her happy. To marry a man she fell in love with, instead of being pushed into a marriage that was expected for the sole purpose of keeping a business in the family. She wanted to live in a place she could afford instead of the monstrosity of a mansion her father had built and her mother had decorated, all to impress the other ridiculously wealthy housewives of River Forest, Chicago.

She was finished with the shallow life from which she'd come. And now that she had the beginnings of a decent-sized nest egg in the bank, it was time to find an apartment of her own. As much as she enjoyed living with Clay, she couldn't rely on his kindness any longer than necessary, and she couldn't stay with him forever. Even if that's what her heart wanted.

She was well past falling in love with a man who'd made her no promises. In fact, he'd all but told her he didn't do long-term, committed relationships. She'd known the deal going in, and while that hadn't bothered her in the beginning, she was gradually coming to realize that she wanted so much more with him.

She also wanted to believe he felt the same. When his guard was down, usually during sex, she caught glimpses of tender, intimate emotions that gave her hope that maybe, possibly, he'd let her into the part of his life he'd closed off to everyone. His dark, troubled past still haunted him, and she wanted to be there for him now to get him past his demons and introduce him to the wonderful future they could share. But so far, he'd shut down any attempt that she made to bring up his childhood. Other than that one revelation about him as a kid looking longingly into the bakery shop window—which nearly broke her heart—he kept all those other secrets and memories on tight lockdown. She wondered if his brothers even knew the extent of his pain.

So for now, she took things one day at a time. And right now, it was all about delivering her latest tasty treat to Clay for him to sample, which was one of her favorite parts of the afternoon. He'd take a break from whatever work he was doing, and while he indulged in a few of her confections, they'd talk about inconsequential things and hang out for a while. No matter how much she desired a deeper conversation and connection, he was keeping her at a distance.

So today, it was time for her to talk to him about her plans for a job that would help her achieve her dreams, and the fact that it was time for her to find a new place to live. She couldn't deny she was excited about reaching for her dreams, but she was equally nervous about how he'd react when she mentioned moving out. Her heart wanted him to rebel against the notion and ask her to stay, but her head warned her against getting her hopes up. This was Clay, the man who was still emotionally shut down, and in all likelihood he'd let her go as planned.

Her stomach churned with nerves as she picked up the plate of cookies and headed downstairs. So far, she hadn't baked the same thing twice, and any leftovers she had, she put in the break room for the employees to try each night. The treats were usually gone within the hour, and everyone wanted more, which she took as a good sign for her future.

Usually, she found Clay in his office, but today he was behind the bar. There were a few racks of various glasses on the counter, and he was writing something down on a notepad. It amazed her how much time and work he put into Kincaid's, but she supposed for him it was a labor of love. Sort of how she felt about the idea of becoming a pastry chef.

Hearing her approach, he glanced up at her and smiled. And yes, her heart literally fluttered in her chest. He was so damned hot and sexy, his T-shirt stretching across his broad chest and toned torso. She'd enjoy him better *out* of the shirt and naked, but for now, she behaved, knowing they had to talk first.

"What are you doing behind the bar?" she asked curiously as she set the plate on the counter.

"Doing a quick check and reorder on the glasses. I do it every few months since they break and I always want to be sure we're well stocked." Setting down his note pad and pen, he came around to her side and eyed the treats on the tray. "What do you have for me today?"

She settled onto a barstool and watched him pick up one of the pastries and look at it with interest. "This is a caramel fleur de sel French macaron."

Clay rolled his eyes, which was what he did whenever she used what he considered a *fancy* name. "Layman's term, please."

She shook her head and grinned. "In words that

you can understand, it's two sweet, meringue-based cookies that are light and chewy, with a whipped caramel cream sandwiched in the center."

"Meringue?" he repeated, raising a brow. "There you go again, using those big words."

"Just try the damn thing," she said, laughing and enjoying the light banter between them, which had become their norm.

Grinning back at her, he took a bite and chewed, then groaned in appreciation. She loved that sound—it was the same sound he made when he was buried deep inside of her, an open expression of pleasure, and it made her happy to be the one to provide that gratification, in whatever form.

"Every day you bake something new. And every day I swear it's my favorite dessert," he said in amusement. "But this macaron thing is like a little bit of heaven in my mouth."

He slipped a hand around the nape of her neck and tipped her head up toward his. "After *you*, of course," he murmured, eyes twinkling wickedly as he sealed his lips against hers and kissed her. Slowly. Leisurely. Thoroughly.

She shivered as his mouth moved over hers seductively, and his tongue tangled lazily with hers until she was breathless and aroused and on the verge of ripping his clothes off and having her way with him right here and now.

But she'd come down today with a purpose, and she needed to follow through on her plan. With a hand pressed to his chest, she gently pushed him back and met his dark, heated gaze that was so very hard to resist.

"I need to talk to you," she said with determination, and wasn't surprised when his entire body language shifted.

He visibly tensed and stepped back, the word "talk" obviously making him wary.

"Talking is overrated," he said in a surprisingly light tone. "Wouldn't you rather go upstairs and have me use my mouth for other things?" he asked in a teasing, sensual tone that contradicted the guarded look in his eyes.

"How about after we talk?" She bit down on her lower lip, knowing she couldn't let him deter her. "It's about something that's important to me," she added softly.

That last part seemingly made all the difference to him, because he gave her a nod and sat down on the chair next to hers so they were facing one another. "What's up?"

"First of all, thank you for letting me use your laptop the last couple of days," she said, wanting to ease into the conversation.

He frowned, obviously not expecting such a casual comment. "Of course. I have my desktop in my office that I use, so it's not a problem. But that can't be what's so urgent."

"No." She folded her hands in her lap to keep them from fidgeting. "I've spent the past week doing a lot of thinking and considering all my options. How do I move forward as a pastry chef? How does someone without experience get a job? And where? And what kind of work environment am I looking for? And I realized that I don't want to work in a restaurant. What I'd like to do is work for a French bakery."

The decision wasn't one she'd come to lightly. She'd really weighed all her options, considering not just the realities but the emotions involved. This was the first time in her life she'd be making her own decision, and she wanted to get it right. And she liked the creativity that came with making tarts and pies and specialty desserts, instead of baking and decorating just cakes.

"I can see you doing that," he said, smiling in support. "Most of things you've made the past two weeks have been French pastries, right?"

She nodded.

"I especially liked that pastry thing you made the other day with the flaky layers of thin crust and vanilla custard," he said.

"The mille-feuille," she replied, knowing exactly what dessert he was referring to.

"Yeah, that one," he said with another teasing eye roll. "Mason went into the break room that night— God only knows for what—and had some of it, too. After eating a slice, he told me that he was going to marry you just so he could keep you barefoot and in the kitchen making him nothing but pastries and pies."

She laughed out loud, because she could easily see

Mason saying something outrageous like that. Over the past two weeks, Clay's middle sibling had made it his mission to flirt with her, and she was pretty sure he only did it to annoy his brother. There was no attraction between the two of them, and she knew Mason's personality well enough by now to know he took great pleasure in yanking Clay's chain.

"What did you say to that?" she asked curiously.

"I told him over my fucking dead body," he said without cracking a smile.

The possessive tone of Clay's voice made her insides quiver. That was yet another thing she'd noticed lately—that Clay was protective and territorial when it came to other men sniffing around her, even his joking brother. Clay was all alpha when it came to her, and she liked it. A lot.

It was ironic that she was so desperate to break free from her parents' hold and become independent, yet she didn't mind when Clay exerted his authority and possessiveness over her. It made her feel warm and mushy inside…wanted…and in a strange way, loved. She shook her head and cleared that thought out of her mind. She liked Clay's control in the bedroom and he liked to exert it. End of story, for him, anyway.

"So, about the French bakery," she continued, getting the conversation back on track. "I contacted someone my mother has hired a few times to make pastries and desserts for various parties at the house. The woman's name is Adeline, and she owns her own

French bakery and catering business in downtown Chicago. I did some research on her business and read reviews on the bakery and catering, all of which were nearly five-star ratings. She has a phenomenal reputation, so I gathered up the nerve and gave her a call."

The slightest of frowns gathered between his brows as he rested his forearm on the counter of the bar. "I had no idea you were looking around for a new job."

He sounded surprised, but whatever else he was feeling, he hid it well.

"I really didn't want to say anything until I knew something was more concrete. For all I knew, I'd hit a dead end. Anyway, when I called, Adeline remembered who I was"—*admittedly, she recognized the Jamieson name first*—"and she wants to interview me next week for a position as a baker."

"That's great," he said, and smiled, genuine happiness for her glimmering in his gaze. "It's exactly what you want, though I have to admit, I'll hate losing such a good cocktail waitress," he said with a wink.

Still, she could tell he was pleased she was following her dreams.

"There's something else I need to tell you." Twisting her hands in her lap, she suddenly realized just how difficult this second part of the talk was going to be. Almost as hard as actually following through on her words.

She swallowed hard and pushed the words past her throat. "I'm going to start looking around for a place of my own. I've taken advantage of your generosity longer than I should have, and though you've been great, it's really past time."

A moment of shock flashed across his features, giving her hope he'd argue against it, but then he quickly schooled his expression into one she could no longer read. "It's not a problem having you stay upstairs," he said, a gruff edge to his voice. "But are you at the point where you can afford a place on your own?"

She heard his doubt, which she understood. He was only thinking about her hourly pay and tips, and even though she had three weeks of savings, it wasn't nearly enough for a first and last month's rent to secure an apartment and still have money left over for living expenses.

"Actually, yes, I can afford my own place." She exhaled a deep breath and told him what she'd done. "I pawned my watch and necklace, so I have more than enough for rent and other necessities, as long as I budget carefully." *Budgeting* was a new concept for her, but she didn't mind if it meant being independent.

He stared at her, the hand on the bar curling into a fist, and she could tell that another round of shock had just hit him and he was trying to process her admission.

"You've been very busy," he finally said, his tone flat.

"I need to start thinking about my future," she said, her throat suddenly thick with too much emotion. "I can't stay here forever."

Their gazes locked, and she wanted him to respond with *yes, you can* so badly her heart ached. And she *would* stay with him if he asked, but that had never been, and probably never would be, an option. Not with a man like Clay, who believed he was meant to be alone. That his ugly past made him unworthy of loving and being loved.

That couldn't be further from the truth. There were so many things to love about Clay. His kindness and the way he took care of everyone around him. He was a decent and generous and selfless human being. He was a man who wouldn't hesitate to slay dragons for the woman lucky enough to stand by his side.

Samantha wished *she* could be that woman.

The back door to the bar opened and closed, intruding on the emotional moment between them and putting an end to their conversation.

Clay exhaled a harsh breath and ran his hand through his hair. "That must be the beer delivery I'm expecting," he said. He moved off the stool and, without a backward glance, headed toward the storeroom.

With an awful pain in her chest, she watched Clay walk away, already feeling him pulling back and retreating from her. And that hurt most of all.

Clay was halfway across the room when a man appeared from the back hallway, and he definitely wasn't dressed like one of the uniformed delivery guys Clay was expecting. The stranger strode into the bar, his gait deliberately slow as he surveyed the area with great interest, his posture slouched in a way that made Samantha's skin crawl. He reminded her more of a gangster or drug addict looking for his next fix than a patron or truck driver.

Clay caught sight of him and came to an abrupt stop, his body stiffening, the muscles in his shoulders and arms bunched tight, as if bracing for a fight. Sudden tension filled the bar and slithered through Samantha, and a surge of fear raced through her, though she couldn't say why.

"Well, well, well," the man with the dark, slicked-back hair drawled with unmistakable arrogance. "If it isn't Clay Kincaid, all grown up with a bar of his very own."

"Get the fuck out of here," Clay said in a low growl so vicious and mean Samantha couldn't believe it had come from the man she knew.

Her panic now justified, Samantha curled her hands round the edge of the bar, the hair on her arms standing on end. She'd never seen or heard this side of Clay before, and it frightened her beyond reason. She wasn't scared *of* him, she was scared *for* him, she thought, watching the scene play out in front of her.

The light in the hallway illuminated the other man's ugly features, and there was absolutely nothing redeeming about his scary, intimidating expression. Greasy hair fell around his face, his nose was crooked, and a long, thick scar started at the corner of his left eye and ended just below his cheekbone. And when he gave Clay a malicious smile, she could see that he was missing teeth, and the ones he did have were dark in color, decaying disgustingly.

Terror kept Samantha frozen on her seat, her insides quaking with fear.

The scary man ran his index finger along that awful-looking scar. "Is that any way to greet an old friend?"

"Get out *now*!" Clay roared, his entire body vibrating with barely suppressed rage.

The other guy had balls of steel, because he didn't so much as flinch. "Not until we have a little chat."

His seedy gaze deliberately slid past Clay and focused on her. He blatantly leered and licked his lips, and Samantha's stomach roiled in disgust.

"Nice piece of ass you got over there," the man taunted.

Lightning fast, Clay's hands shot out, shoving so hard against the guy's shoulder the man grunted and stumbled backward, nearly falling on his ass. He caught himself just in time and straightened. Clay stepped toward him to do more damage, but the other man drew a switchblade, and Clay stopped short.

"You always were a stupid little fuck," the man spat viciously, his eyes narrowed to slits. "Touch me again and I won't hesitate to gut you, just as I should have done all those years ago. And your whore over there can watch you bleed out."

Samantha sucked in a breath, tears coming to her eyes, her throat full and burning. She'd never felt so helpless at the thought of anything happening to Clay.

"Go upstairs, Samantha," Clay ordered in a shockingly steady voice, though he never took his eyes off the knife-wielding man in front of him.

Without hesitation, she jumped off the chair and did as she was told, hating that she was about to leave Clay alone with a man who was clearly an unstable monster.

She had to walk past the standoff in order to head down the hallway to the stairs, and as she did, the nauseating scent of body order combined with whiskey and bad breath made her stomach lurch.

Her eyes connected with the man's, his gaze pitch-black, as if he had no soul. His smile was just as evil. "Don't worry, I won't stab lover boy unless he gives me a reason to," he sneered at her as she rushed past.

As soon as she reached the door heading up to the apartment, she wrenched it open, not trusting herself to glance back at Clay. Despite her legs feeling like Jell-O, she managed to run up the stairs, the tears she'd been holding back rushing forward, and she sobbed as she dug through her purse for her phone.

With shaking hands, she called one of the very few people she'd put into her new contact list. Katrina.

Samantha was a blubbering mess by the time the other woman answered her phone, much too cheerful when Samantha was falling apart. "Send Mason over to the bar immediately. There's a man here who is threatening to kill Clay."

Then she disconnected the line and called the police.

# Chapter Twelve

WITH SAMANTHA GONE and safe upstairs, Clay ignored the nausea churning in his stomach as he stared down his worst nightmare—the man who'd made his and his brothers' childhood a living fucking hell. The vile piece of shit who'd kept their mother doped up on meth and pimped her out to any random stranger for cash and narcotics, until their mother was arrested and sent to prison for an eighteen-month sentence for drug possession and prostitution.

That's when the real horror had begun for Clay and his brothers.

Wyatt Dawson was pure evil. A man without a conscience or morals, and that made him a dangerous son of a bitch. And he'd stopped by to *talk*, which Clay suspected meant he was here for one of two things: extortion or blackmail, because that's how corrupt men like Wyatt operated.

"You and I have nothing to talk about, asshole," Clay said bitterly.

"Oh, but I think we do." Wyatt smiled insolently, but despite the man's outward bravado, Clay caught a hint of desperation in his gaze. "I need some cash. Fifty grand, to be exact, and you're going to provide it by the end of the week."

Clay barked out an incredulous laugh. "I don't have that kind of fucking money," he lied, hoping like hell that Wyatt hadn't somehow found out about the inheritance from Jerry. "And even if I did, you are the last person on earth I'd *give* it to, so get the fuck out."

"Not so fast," Wyatt said, much too patiently as he twirled that sharp, glinting knife between his fingers like a threat. "You *will* give me that money, unless you want something to happen to this bar, or more importantly, that sweet, blonde thing with the wide, innocent eyes. She'd fetch at *least* fifty grand on the black market."

White-hot rage boiled through Clay's veins, and it took every ounce of restraint he had in his body *not* to wrap his hands around the fucker's neck and choke him out. "I should have fucking killed you while I had the chance," he spat in a low, feral tone.

"Yes, you should have. But you didn't, and here we are, having a nice little family reunion." Wyatt smirked. "Fifty grand in cash, and you have three days to make it happen."

Clay caught another quick pass of anxiety on Wyatt's face, leading Clay to believe that the other man was tangled up with someone or something as evil and sadistic as himself. "How about I just let natural selection take its course," Clay goaded, because he had a damn good hunch that if he didn't come through with the money, whomever Wyatt owed it to would wipe him off the face of the earth.

*Wouldn't that be poetic justice?*

"Do *not* fuck with me," Wyatt snarled like a rabid dog as he touched the tip of his switchblade to Clay's chest, the wild and crazy look in his eyes edged with a hint of panic. "Make it happen, or you won't like the consequences. I'll be in touch." Wyatt turned around and left the way he'd come in, out the back delivery door.

Once he was gone, Clay walked over to the nearest chair and dropped into it. His heart was still pounding so erratically it felt as though it would burst out of his chest, and he scrubbed his hand down his face, waiting for the adrenaline rushing through him to subside.

"Fuck," he muttered, feeling as though his entire world had just been shaken and dumped upside down.

In the past hour, he'd been delivered a one-two punch. He'd been reeling from Samantha's announcement that she was leaving soon, and then Satan himself had been resurrected from his childhood. He honestly didn't know which one was worse or more painful. Dealing with Wyatt and his demands or knowing that the woman who'd come to mean so much to him would walk out of his life.

After the confrontation with Wyatt, it was abundantly clear exactly why Samantha didn't belong in his world. One tainted by hatred and violence—ugly, vile things that should never, ever touch Samantha in any way. *And they had.*

A deep, dark groan escaped his throat. What a goddamn mess, and now Samantha was caught in the middle of his horrific past that was colliding with the present. He didn't doubt for a minute that Wyatt's threat toward Samantha was real. The man was capable of all sorts of heinous crimes, and the fact that he'd mentioned human trafficking told Clay he probably had a hand in it, too. He gagged, sick and furious as hell that this man was still hurting other people. Other women.

One of those wouldn't be Samantha. There was no way in fucking hell he'd ever let Wyatt touch her, let alone come near her again. He'd kill the other man or die himself protecting the woman he loved.

His stomach flipped in his belly as the word popped into his head so easily, so quickly, so damned naturally, he grew dizzy. Clay had sworn he didn't know what love was, let alone what it felt like, yet he understood with certainty that Samantha was the very first woman, the *only* woman, he wanted in his life. And not just as a temporary diversion.

*Shit.*

The back delivery door slammed open, and Clay jumped to his feet, his hands instinctively balling into fists to defend himself if he needed to.

"Where the fuck is he?" Mason bellowed like an

enraged and reckless bull. He charged into the bar area, followed closely by a more reserved but still clearly worked up Levi, who was in uniform and had his service pistol drawn.

Relief poured through Clay, and he wasn't at all surprised that his brothers *knew* who'd been here after Samantha had called them for backup. She'd have his back in any way she could. He only thanked God she'd chosen the safest, smartest route.

"Wyatt's gone," he said, confirming what they suspected.

Mason looked around, his expression fierce. "Where's Samantha?" He demanded. "Is she okay?"

Clay nodded, realizing just how much they'd *all* come to care for her in such a short time, especially Mason. There were very few people his middle brother was protective of, and Samantha was clearly one of them.

"She was down here when Wyatt came in and saw him at his finest," he said in disgust.

"Fucking asshole," Mason said of the man who'd tormented all three of them.

Clay couldn't argue. "I sent her upstairs as soon as I could." Once again, he thanked God that she'd listened to him. "I'm assuming she called you."

"She called Katrina," Mason muttered. "She insisted on coming with us, so I sent her up to the apartment the back way so Samantha wouldn't be alone."

Knowing that she had someone to talk to, to keep

her calm, enabled Clay to remain down here with his brothers. "Thanks."

Levi, still in his quiet, serious mode, secured his weapon back into the holster at his side. "After all these years, what the hell did he want?"

"Money. Fifty grand, to be exact," Clay told his brothers. "Somehow, he found out I owned the bar. He obviously needs a quick infusion of cash, and he expects to get it from me."

"Fucker!" Mason smacked a fist into his other palm, the anger and energy vibrating off him nearly palpable. "You should have killed him, Clay. You know I would have helped you bury the body or feed him to the sharks."

Clay knew that Mason wasn't joking, but the way Mr. Law Enforcement crossed his arms over his chest and glared at their hotheaded brother told them that *killing Wyatt* wasn't an option. Levi was a by-the-book cop all the way.

Mason sneered at Levi. "You're such a fucking kill-joy."

Levi shrugged. "I'm just trying to keep a pretty boy like you out of prison and from becoming some guy's bitch."

Mason huffed out a breath and went to the bar. "I need a goddamn drink."

Knowing the three of them had a lot to talk about, Clay sat down at one of the tables, and Levi took the seat next to him, his gaze concerned.

"You okay?" Levi asked.

Clay couldn't believe that just a few weeks ago, he and Levi had had a heated conversation about Wyatt, and now he was back in their lives. How ironic was that?

"I'll be fine." It was the best assurance he could give his brother right now, until they figured out a *legal* way out of this mess.

They waited for Mason to return, and when he did, he had a full bottle of premium bourbon tucked under one arm and was carrying two shot glasses and a drink for Levi in his hands. He set the shot glasses on the table, followed by the liquor, then handed Levi the other glass filled nearly to the brim.

"I thought you could use something stronger than your normal pansy-ass spritzer," Mason said in a mocking tone. "Orange juice, straight up."

"Always a comedian, aren't you?" Levi drawled and downed half the glass in one long gulp while Mason poured the Knob Creek Single Barrel Reserve into the two shot glasses.

Clay tossed back the bourbon the same time that Mason did, then got down to business. "There's more I need to tell you two." Both brothers immediately gave him their undivided attention. "Wyatt gave me three days to come up with the cash, and he seemed desperate, so I'm assuming that he's in some kind of trouble."

"Yeah, well, he can rot in hell for all I care," Mason said, already consuming his second shot.

When Clay didn't respond right away, Mason

frowned at him. "You're not thinking about giving him the money, are you?" he asked incredulously.

"It's not my first option, but he threatened Samantha," Clay told them, his stomach knotting all over again at the other man's intimidation tactics. "Said if he didn't get the cash by the end of the week, he'd get fifty grand from Samantha on the black market."

"Jesus," Mason breathed in disgust. "The fucker is now into human trafficking?"

"That's what he implied, and we all know what Wyatt is capable of," Clay replied.

His brothers nodded their agreement, and Levi continued to listen to the conversation in that introspective way of his. Clay had no doubts Levi's sharp mind was working to figure out a legitimate solution to their problem, and he hoped to hell that he came up with one soon.

"Bottom line, I can't keep Samantha locked in my apartment forever to protect her. And if I don't give Wyatt what he wants, and anything happened to Samantha because of me, it would *kill* me." Just the thought of anyone hurting her made a sharp-as-a-knife pain stab through Clay's heart.

"Nothing is going to happen to her." Levi finally spoke up.

Clay had always been the caretaker in the family, the protector, and for the first time ever, he found himself looking to Levi for advice, hoping and praying that his youngest sibling would truly be able to find a way to put an end to this insanity.

"What do you have in mind?" Clay prompted.

"Let me run his name through the system and see what comes up," Levi suggested. "I'm sure he has a rap sheet a mile long, which doesn't do us any good, but there might be an outstanding warrant for his arrest. When he shows up again, we can take him into custody and charge him for blackmail and extortion, too."

"So he can get another slap on the wrist and be out on the streets in a few weeks?" Mason scoffed.

Understanding flickered in Levi's gaze. "I know it's not ideal, but give me a day to see what I can come up with, and we'll go from there."

"I like my idea of feeding him to the sharks much better," Mason muttered irritably.

Clay agreed that Levi's scenario wasn't the permanent solution that he'd been hoping for. Sooner or later, Wyatt would get out of jail and come after Clay. Or worse, Samantha.

He glanced at Levi. "I don't care what happens to me, but while this is all going down, I need to know that Samantha is safe at all times."

"Consider it done," Levi said with a nod. "I'll get a security detail on her ASAP.

"Thank you." Other than making sure that he did everything in his power to protect Samantha, there was nothing else Clay could do. And he hated feeling so helpless when he preferred being a man of action. The gnawing worry for Samantha was something new, too. Something, he realized, he'd gone out of his way to avoid ever feeling. But Samantha had barreled into his life, filling his dark, monotonous days with color and light. She gave him something to look forward to each day. Hope, he realized, was something new to him, too.

But, as he'd always known, she didn't belong in his life for long. She deserved so much more, so much better than he could ever give. And hadn't Wyatt's sudden appearance and threats proven that in spades?

Which was why—once this mess with Wyatt was finished—the most selfless thing he could do for her was let her go.

SAMANTHA TOSSED AND turned in bed, mentally exhausted but unable to fall into a deep sleep. It was nearly two in the morning, and while she'd drifted off a few times since lying down, she'd been jolted awake by terrifying images of the man who'd come into the bar the previous afternoon. Horrific nightmares of him stabbing Clay in the stomach while Samantha sat helplessly by, watching him die.

After Clay had sent her upstairs and she'd called for help, she'd gone back down and listened at the door. And that's when she'd heard the threats the man had issued if he didn't get *fifty thousand dollars*—money Clay insisted he didn't have—in the next few days. She'd been included in that threat, but she couldn't bring herself to think about that. All she could concern herself with was Clay.

Not for the first time, tears and emotions jammed in her throat. The fear of something bad happening to Clay was real—she'd seen the evil look in the other man's eyes. And she couldn't just do nothing. She couldn't risk him seriously hurting or killing Clay. Just her brief glimpse of the man from a distance convinced her he was capable of that kind of violence.

She blinked back the burn of tears, more memories returning. The cavalry had arrived soon after she'd called—Mason and Levi, along with Katrina, who'd stayed with her in the apartment and calmed her down. Finally, Clay had come up much later to check on Samantha and let her know that there was an undercover cop in an unmarked car in the parking lot outside, to make sure she was safe at all times.

He'd also informed her that he didn't want her working in the bar for a few days, and then he was gone, storming out of the apartment and headed God knew where. After a while, Katrina had had to leave, and Samantha had spent the rest of the afternoon and evening alone, unable to even focus on a TV show, since she'd had a continuous running loop in her head that kept replaying the entire confrontation with Clay and the man. And the end result she'd conjured in her mind had her nearly sobbing every single time.

Staring at the ceiling in the dark, her mind working overtime, she finally figured out a plan. Tears trailed down the sides of her face because she knew what she had to do. The decision hadn't been an easy one to make, because she understood what the repercussions of her choices would be. But when it came to making sure *Clay* was safe, she would sacrifice herself, her life, her freedom. Even her own dreams. And she didn't kid herself that she was overreacting. Because once she asked her father for the money Clay needed, the price wouldn't just be the life she'd fought so hard to create. The cost would be giving up Clay himself. Her father would see to that.

Another half hour had passed when she *finally* heard Clay come into the apartment. She waited for him to walk into the bedroom, but it didn't happen. She gave him another fifteen minutes before tossing the covers off to take matters into her own hands.

It was obvious that he was avoiding her again, but they needed to talk about what had happened at the bar, whether he liked it or not. Harder still, she needed to tell him she was going to go home, which brought on another surge of waterworks. There was no way she could leave without him finding out, not when he had her so well protected. And besides, he'd been so good to her she owed him the truth about where she was going—if not exactly why. The fifty thousand he needed would arrive after she was gone, allowing him to get that awful man out of his life.

She couldn't do it any other way. If she told him about getting him the money now, he'd fight her. A proud man like Clay wouldn't like accepting a handout any more than he'd want her bailing him out. She only hoped that when he received the cash, he'd take it and know that she'd done it because she loved him.

Without turning on the bedroom light, she quietly opened the door and glanced around the adjoining living room. The entire place was dark except for the beam of moonlight coming in through the kitchen window that illuminated Clay's form. He was facing away from her, shirtless and just in his jeans. As she silently approached, she could see that he had his hands braced on the counter and his head hung forward, as if he was exhausted and defeated. It was the latter emotion that made her heart ache for him.

She moved closer, intending to slip her hands around his waist and hug him from behind so he didn't feel so alone, but she stopped short when she saw at least two dozen round scars all over his back, which were about the diameter of a pencil. Shock rippled through her, and that's when she realized that despite all the times they'd been together and all the times he'd been without a shirt, she'd never seen his bare back before—something he'd obviously and deliberately kept from her gaze so he didn't have to explain how he'd gotten those burn marks, which she suspected were from the tip of a smoldering cigarette.

She reached a hand out to touch his back. The moment the tips of her fingers grazed one of those scars, he spun around so fast she gasped, and before she could exhale a breath, he locked her wrist in his strong hand. His expression was dark and fierce, his gaze glittering with such savage intensity it was as if he didn't recognize her. He looked like a man emotionally tormented and broken. This normally undaunted man who was so strong for everyone else and never showed any weakness now looked stripped bare. And she wanted to do whatever it took to soothe his anguish and pain.

"Clay," she said, loud and firm enough to snap him out of whatever memories or trance he'd been lost in. "It's me. Samantha."

He blinked in the dim light, his gaze clearing and focusing on her face as recognition chased across his features. "Jesus," he swore harshly, and released her hand, though the grim frown remained, as did the tension stiffening his body. "What the hell are you doing up?"

"I couldn't sleep," she said, refusing to recoil from the snap in his voice. "Just like you."

"Go back to bed, Samantha," he said gruffly.

She swallowed hard and remained standing right where she was. After what had happened today, his walls were a mile high. And even though she knew it wouldn't change anything about her decision to leave in the morning, she wanted that guard down between them now. Just this once. She wanted him to trust her with his pain, with all the horrific things he'd suffered through. All the horrible things she knew he never talked about because the memories were too terrible to bear.

Determination made her brave, and she lifted her chin to let him know she wasn't going anywhere until he talked. "Tell me how you got those scars on your back."

His jaw clenched at her insistence, and a spark of fury ignited in his gaze. "It doesn't fucking matter."

That's what *he* honestly believed, but she wanted— *no, needed*—him to know that she cared for him. Deeply. Irrevocably. "Every single thing about you matters to me," she said, unable to stop the rise of emotion that made her voice quiver. "Including how you got those scars."

"Let it go, Samantha," he warned darkly.

A wiser woman would have hightailed it out of the kitchen and back to the safety of the bedroom, but there was nothing about Clay that she feared, except losing him, and that was going to happen anyway. Standing inches away from her, he was like a brewing volcano about to erupt and unleash a firestorm of emotional fury.

She instinctively knew that all those years of suppressing a childhood of suffering were trying to claw their way out, and when all that overwhelming agony detonated, it was going to be brutal and violent.

But like a festering wound, he had to be cleansed before he could heal.

So she pushed a little harder. "Was it that man who came in today? Did he hurt you?"

Clay fisted his hands at his sides, his breathing deepening. "Leave. It. Alone."

She couldn't, because that meant leaving *him* alone, with all the pain. "You don't have to keep everything bottled so tight inside of you."

His stare was hard and cold. "My past is dark, twisted, and ugly, and the last thing I want to do is put those gruesome images in your head that don't need to be there," he snapped, but the sudden heat in his eyes was at odds with his harsh tone, making her shiver with longing. "Leave me alone before I do something we'll both regret."

The sexual undercurrents in his tone made it clear what that *something* was. Despite his attempts to push her away, there was no mistaking he wanted her. And if the only outlet she could give him was a physical one, then she'd grant him the permission to use her body to slake his emotional needs.

"I will never regret anything I've done with you. *Ever*," she said, hoping he remembered those words long after she was gone.

Before he could say anything else, she boldly closed the distance between them, wrapped her arms around his neck so her body was pressed tight against him, and lifted her mouth to his.

The touch of their lips was all it took for Clay to come unhinged. With a raspy, guttural groan, his hands came up and gripped her hair near the roots, and she welcomed the slight sting of pain. He pulled her head back and slanted his mouth across hers so he was in complete control of the kiss, and she had no problem letting him take charge. This carnal, primitive mating was all about him, and she'd surrender to *anything* he wanted or needed from her.

He pressed her back against the nearest counter,

his muscled body pinning her there while his tongue thrust deep and his mouth ravaged hers until her lips felt swollen and bruised. His chest rose and fell rapidly as his breathing escalated and his hunger for her intensified. She pivoted her hips, a soft, needy sound escaping her lips, a sensual plea for him to satisfy the ache building and expanding inside of her.

Releasing her hair, he shoved his hands beneath her long sleep shirt and cupped her ass in his palms, raising her and pressing her sex against the enormous bulge straining behind the fly of his jeans. She rolled her pelvis against his, and a huge shudder shook his strong frame. He slid his hands down her thighs and lifted her until she was able to wrap her legs tight and secure around his waist.

They both groaned into each other's mouth as his rigid cock rubbed and pressed against the wet silk covering her sex. He ground his hips upward, hard and brutally, again and again, fucking her through the clothing separating their bodies, determined to achieve the pleasure he sought, clothing be damned. Fisting her hands in his hair, she arched her back, so hungry for Clay, and even more desperate to feel all that firm, solid flesh filling her so exquisitely. So perfectly, in a way no man ever would again.

With a sharp hiss of breath, he ripped his mouth from hers and buried his face against her neck, his hot, damp lips near her ear. "*Samantha...*" he groaned, his voice desolate and emotionally shattered. "I need you so fucking bad."

The admission nearly broke her heart. A man like Clay didn't want to *need* anyone, yet he was letting her in the only way he knew how, allowing her to see a vulnerable side that truly left him emotionally gutted and defenseless.

She wouldn't take that gift for granted. "Take me any way you want," she whispered back. "I'm yours." And no matter what happened after tonight, she knew she would always belong to this man. Heart and soul.

His groan was filled with pure relief. With her arms and legs anchored around him, he carried her into the bedroom, laid her back on the mattress, and pulled off her nightshirt and panties in quick succession. He stepped back, stripping off his jeans and briefs. After retrieving a condom from the nightstand and sheathing himself, he moved onto the bed, between her already spread legs.

He brushed the tips of his fingers reverently through her soft, wet folds, his tender caress so at odds with the possessive heat blazing in his wild eyes that told her this joining was going to be demanding and greedy. That once he was buried deep inside of her, it was going to be a relentless, merciless ride to the finish.

The thought made her stomach quiver and her nipples peak into hard, needy points. She was already drenched and sensitive, her body so attuned to his touch. Another dip and swirl of his skillful fingers, and she gripped the comforter in her hands and shuddered, knowing it wasn't going to take much at all for her to come.

Once he was assured that she was ready for him, he lifted her legs up, resting her ankles on his shoulders. He aligned the engorged tip of his cock against her opening and leaned all the way over her until his arms were braced on either side of her head. With his dark, glittering eyes locked on hers, he reared back slightly and drove inside her with one hard, ruthless thrust.

She sucked in a shocked breath—at the initial twinge of pain and surprisingly tight fit, and the way her hips naturally tilted up to take him so impossibly deep. She was pinned beneath him, her body completely open to him, completely *his*, no doubt, just as he intended. This unconventional position gave him all the power, all the leverage he needed to take her *any way he wanted*.

His taut body trembled, and she realized he was holding back. And she instinctively knew why. "There is nothing you can do to hurt me, and I'm not going to break," she assured him huskily, giving him what he needed to hear. "Fuck me, Clay. Fuck me hard, because it's what I want, too."

Her words made him snap, and he started to move, driving into her, again and again. His hips surging faster and faster. Pounding harder and harder. Sliding deeper and deeper, each time dragging the head of his cock against sensitive nerve endings just inside her channel until the sensation had her trying to shift in counterpoint to Clay's aggressive thrusts. She couldn't breathe, couldn't move. She could only let the climax build, as Clay's control finally shattered.

He bared his teeth with an animalistic growl, his hips *pumping, pumping, pumping,* until the relentless friction set off her release. Her entire body splintered from the inside out, exquisite sensation taking her over the edge and keeping her there. She moaned and tipped her head back, feeling her internal muscles continue to flutter, tighten, and squeeze around his cock as she came and came and came—so long and hard she couldn't hold back her scream of pleasure.

With one last brutal thrust, he followed her over with a hoarse shout, his body jerking hard, releasing not only his orgasm but, she hoped, his demons, as well.

It was the last gift she could give him, and she wanted it to matter.

# Chapter Thirteen

THE CALM AFTER the storm. That's what it felt like as Clay lay on his back on the bed with a warm, naked Samantha curled into the crook of his arm and her head resting on his shoulder. While he was still worried about the situation with Wyatt, the anger and barely suppressed rage he'd been carrying with him all day and night were now just a dull ache in his chest. *Thank God.*

Samantha had gotten him through one of the worst days in recent memory, had given herself over to him so selflessly, her body and, he suspected, even more. She'd surrendered everything to him, not thinking twice about allowing him to slake his primal need inside her, to release all the pain he'd kept buried since he was a kid because he didn't know jack shit about how to deal with his emotions. It had been so much easier to suppress the pain and misery, despite the dark memories lingering just below the surface, always there, silently festering, just waiting for the one trigger to cause an eruption when the past resurfaced again.

Seeing Wyatt after all these years, remembering all the horrific things he'd endured at the man's hands, and him threatening Samantha, had been the catalyst, causing him to unleash all the ugliness in a firestorm of rage and bitterness that had threatened to consume him. And it would have, if Samantha hadn't come out of the bedroom and been strong *for* him. She'd been the anchor he'd so desperately needed to keep him grounded when he'd been so damn close to losing his mind and fracturing in two.

She'd asked about the scars on his back, and after everything Samantha had just given him, along with the fact that Wyatt had her in his sights, she deserved to know the truth. About everything. But first, he owed her an apology for being so rough on her, for taking her like a fucking animal.

With her head resting against his shoulder, he lifted his hand and gently stroked his fingers through her soft, silky hair. "I'm sorry," he said, his voice raspier than he'd expected it to be.

"I'm not," she replied quietly, understanding the reason he was apologizing before he could even explain. "It was what you needed, and I'm grateful that I was here for you." Her warm breath drifted across his chest as she spoke.

He was grateful, too, more than she'd ever know.

God, she knew him so well. Had known what he'd needed even before he had. "Then I guess what I should say is thank you."

Before she could respond to that, he quickly pushed out the next words so he couldn't change his mind. "You asked about the scars on my back and what happened back when I was a kid."

"Yes. Will you tell me?" She was quiet and hopeful but not demanding.

He realized she was giving him a choice, and for the first time in his life, he found himself *wanting* to share the most personal, private side of himself with someone. With Samantha. And so he did, starting from the beginning.

"My mother was a crack whore and a prostitute," he said, bracing himself for some kind of negative reaction from Samantha—flinching, shuddering, something to indicate her disgust. But the only thing she did was rest her hand on his chest, right over his beating heart, as if she needed that emotional connection to him as much as he needed her.

He swallowed the thick knot in his throat and continued. "Mason, Levi, and I, we all have different fathers. Each time our mother got pregnant, it was with a different john, so we don't even know who our fathers were. We never had a man's influence in our lives. But there were many jerk-offs who lived with us in our one-bedroom apartment, and they were all drug addicts like our mother," he said, unable to withhold the disgust he harbored. "And since she was never aware or conscious enough to take care of us kids, I took on the role at a very early age."

"That must've been hard," she murmured, her hand still lingering over his heart.

He didn't acknowledge just how difficult it had been. "I was six when Levi was born, and even then, I was the one who made sure he had his bottle, and I changed his diapers the best I could. I made cereal and sandwiches for me and Mason—at least when we had food in the house, but a lot of times we went to bed hungry."

She lifted her head and met his gaze, her blue eyes filled with compassion and a flicker of anger, too. "Why didn't social services step in?"

He wasn't surprised someone as pure and untouched as Samantha still believed in the system. "We lived in the projects, and nobody cared about what happened with their neighbors. Nobody noticed, so my mother was never reported. And in her lucid moments, when I complained, my mother instilled the fear of God in me, warning me that if I told anyone that she was rarely home or that we had no food, social services would come by—to take us away and split the three of us up forever."

"That's awful," she said, her voice an aching whisper.

He shrugged. "That was my life." Exhaling a deep breath, he gently pressed a hand to the back of her head and brought her cheek back to rest on his chest, and continued to stroke her hair. It was much easier to talk to her about his past without looking into her sad, somber eyes.

"So at the age of six, you became the caretaker for your brothers."

"Mmm-hmm. And I went to school because I had to or someone would notice and they'd split us up. And I was a good kid because I was always so afraid that if I did anything bad, I'd lose my brothers forever."

"They were lucky to have you," she murmured.

He shrugged. "I did what I had to do. I raised Mason and Levi the best I could and tried to keep them out of trouble. Then, when I was fifteen, my mother got involved with Wyatt. He moved in and kept her even more doped up on drugs, pimping her out for cash while running his own seedy side businesses. And while she was out at night prostituting herself, Wyatt would terrorize us."

A full-body shudder racked his frame at the memory, but he'd started this, and he intended to finish. "He was an abusive, sadistic prick who preyed on the weak, and because my brothers were still so young and couldn't defend themselves, I'd deflect as much of the abuse as I could, turning it my way. And one of the things that Wyatt liked to do the most to assert his authority was to pin me down on the floor and press the burning end of his cigarette against my back, until it literally burned a hole in my flesh."

Bile rose in his throat at the hellish memory, while beside him, Samantha stiffened and a soft choking sound escaped her throat. But Clay wasn't done. "The sick bastard would get off on my screaming. The more I squirmed or cried, the more he'd laugh and press the cigarette harder and longer against my skin." He closed his eyes, seeking to escape the memories he lived with every single day. "But at least he didn't do it to my brothers," he said, repeating the words that had gotten him through the pain and allowed him to take the abuse. "And though there were times when Mason and Levi watched helplessly, I'd warned them *not* to get involved."

Samantha made another small sound of distress. She wrapped an arm around his midsection and cuddled closer to his side, holding him tight and silently comforting him. Her warmth and silent understanding soothed his frayed emotions, enabling him to go on. He felt like the story would never end, just as he'd felt while living the horror.

"This went on for months, until one day our mother was arrested for drug possession and solicitation. Since it was her fifth offense on various charges, she was sent to state prison for eighteen months." He absently rubbed his hand along the arm still secured across his abdomen. "I don't know the legalities, but somehow that stupid bitch was able to appoint Wyatt as our guardian until she was released, and during that time, the abuse only got worse."

Samantha's head abruptly snapped up, her expression horrified. "Why would she do that to you and your brothers?" she asked, appalled.

"I honestly don't know." And he never would. "But I'm guessing it made the most sense to her drug-addled brain. He lived with us anyway, and her kids had never been a priority or a concern. Her only worry had always been how she was going to get her next fix."

"What happened to her?" Samantha asked.

"She'd served three months of her sentence when she had a fatal stroke and died. Probably because of the drugs. Anyway, that's when Wyatt decided that we were now his *property*, to do with as he pleased."

Samantha stared at him, her eyes wide and horror-filled. Someone like her, who'd been born into wealth and privilege, had never been exposed to such harsh realities, or the cruel reality of living in poverty.

"The thought of Wyatt being our legal guardian, until each one of us reached the age of eighteen, scared the shit out of me. I knew he'd do everything he could to intimidate and corrupt Mason and Levi. I was afraid he'd turn them on to drugs, pimp them out, or worse. So one day, I stole a butcher knife from a store. Just in case."

Samantha was watching him so silently and intently he had to glance away, unsure of whether he could admit to the rest. It had been the worst night of his life, and he hated that he'd had to resort to such violence. Yet he'd do it all over again to protect his brothers.

She touched his jaw and turned his face back to hers. "Tell me," she said softly, her gaze imploring him to trust her with his past, his pain.

So he did. "One day, I came home and Wyatt had Levi cornered. He'd already backhanded him a few times. I told Levi to run and he did. He locked himself in the bathroom, and as soon as he was out of the way, Wyatt came after me like I knew he would. I pulled out the knife. There was so much fury running through me and I was so amped up that I swore I was going to kill the fucker. Back then, Wyatt was damned strong, and he came close to overpowering me." Samantha sucked in a breath, remaining silent, waiting for the rest.

Clay swallowed hard. "Somehow, I managed to push back, and I used the blade to slice a deep cut along the side of his face."

She blinked at him in disbelief. "You gave him that scar?"

"Yes." He didn't feel any pride in the memory. "I stabbed him in the arm, too, and it was enough for Wyatt to realize that he couldn't screw with us anymore, and he finally left."

Yet Wyatt was back in their lives, which once more told Clay he must be desperate. But Clay wasn't. As a teenager, he wouldn't have hesitated to slaughter the asshole if it meant keeping his brothers safe. But now he had way too much to lose to go to prison for the rest of his life for murdering the scumbag.

"Wyatt knew I was serious, and he left, and we haven't seen him until now, when he obviously needs cash to get himself out of some kind of trouble."

Samantha's mind spun as she tried to process everything Clay had told her, unable to imagine all that he'd been through as a kid. Her heart felt torn in shreds, knowing that he'd endured so much abuse yet never hesitated to step up and be strong for Mason and Levi.

"Your brothers were still so young when that happened," she said, curious to know how Clay had kept them together without any adult supervision or financial means. "So what did you do once Wyatt was gone?"

"Mason was twelve and Levi was ten. No way was I going to lose them to foster care," he said gruffly. "So I did everything possible to make sure that didn't happen. For two years, until I turned eighteen, I worked any kind of job I could to pay the rent and utilities and remain under the radar. Mowing lawns. Bagging groceries. Collecting cans and bottles and recycling them for cash. I'd even dig through dumpsters for food or other things we needed. And then Jerry hired me here at the bar and gave me a weekly paycheck. Levi was a good kid who did exactly as I said and made sure he stayed out of trouble. But Jesus Christ, Mason was a goddamn hellion," he said with a self-derisive laugh.

She smiled at Clay. "So, he started at a young age, huh?"

"Yeah." Clay sighed heavily. "With everything that happened, Mason had a lot of anger inside of him. And after our mother died and Wyatt left, he got worse. He tested my authority constantly and made it difficult to keep all of us off the radar, until I turned eighteen and could apply for guardianship for them both. And with Mason fourteen, those teenage years were a nightmare. He was such a fucking handful," he said, humor in his voice now that his brother was a grown man and no longer his responsibility. "He was constantly sneaking out in the middle of the night, hanging with the wrong crowd, getting involved in drugs. When he was seventeen, he was arrested for spraying graffiti on public and private property, and because I knew he was headed down a really bad path, I didn't try to stop it when he was sent to juvie for six months."

Samantha could easily imagine what a delinquent Mason had been as a teen. "I think he turned out okay." Thanks to his brother's diligence and guidance.

"Meh," Clay said in a teasing tone, then grew serious once again. "I really think that Mason constantly tested and defied me because he believed that I was going to leave him like our mother had. She might not have been part of our life in any way that mattered, but she was our mother. We didn't have a father, and not knowing who his dad was, knowing that it was some random john our mother had screwed for a hit messed with Mason's head, too. Still does, I think."

"You did the best you could," she said, gently trailing her fingers up and down his chest. "Both of your brothers turned out to be good men because of everything you did for them."

He scrubbed a hand along the stubble on his jaw, suddenly looking tired and weary. "Except here we are, facing the man who fucked all of us up, when I thought we'd never see him again."

A very dangerous man demanding a staggering amount of money that Clay didn't have. The reminder made Samantha's chest tighten and ripped her heart in two because of the decision she'd had to make. The only choice she *could* make to be sure that Clay, and his brothers, remained safe. Even if it meant leaving the one man who made her feel whole and complete. The man she loved with every fiber of her being and would never see again after tomorrow morning.

Clay frowned up at her, and that's when Samantha realized that her eyes had filled with tears. And there was no way to hide them or blink them back.

"Hey, what's with this?" he asked in concern as he wiped away one of the drops with his thumb as it spilled over her lashes. "Are you okay?"

She swallowed hard, pushing back an even bigger wave of emotion. "Yeah. It's just been a long day and night," she said with a tremulous smile.

He'd been through the emotional wringer, and she didn't think now was the right time to tell him she'd be leaving in the morning. And selfishly, she wanted one last night in his arms. Because she didn't want him asking any more questions, she kissed him in order to distract him and, more importantly, to keep herself from thinking about a life without Clay in it.

❖    ❖    ❖

WHEN CLAY CAME out of the bathroom the following morning after taking a shower, dressed in just a pair of jeans, he found Samantha setting all her clothes and personal items on the bed, then transferring each pile into a large shopping bag. She wouldn't look at him, and a frisson of unease coursed through him.

"Samantha, why are you packing?" he asked, wondering if she'd already found a place to live, which didn't make sense. She'd just brought up the idea of moving out, then Wyatt had appeared. There was no way she had anywhere to go yet. And even if she did, he wasn't letting her out of this apartment without some kind of security or protection.

When she didn't reply immediately and just continued to pack her things, his concern increased. He closed the distance between them and gently grabbed her arm, forcing her to face him. "Samantha?"

She lifted her chin, and he immediately recognized that show of determination, but it was the anguish in her eyes that made his chest tighten with anxiety. The kind that came with knowing that his entire world was about to disintegrate and there wasn't a damn thing he could do about it.

"I'm going home," she said, her voice raspy with emotion and pain.

Reeling in shock, he dropped her arm, feeling something substantial crumble deep inside of him. *She was leaving him*, and he was hit with a kind of desperation he'd never known before. The desperation to make her *stay*. With him. Forever.

And how fucking selfish was that considering everything he'd put her through in the past twenty-four hours alone?

"So you're just giving up what *you* want and fought so hard for?"

She closed her eyes for a moment, gathering her composure, then picked up a folded pile of clothes and set it inside the sack. "It's what I need to do."

No other explanation, and he didn't have the right to demand one. He clenched his hands at his sides to keep from touching her again. He understood her need to hightail it out of here and get far away from him. Her life had been threatened, and last night he'd used her in a harsh way she didn't deserve, then he'd unloaded all his emotional shit on her. Stuff that never should have seen the light of day, never mind touched Samantha.

He'd always known his past was tainted with nothing but gruesome ugliness, and for that reason, from the moment she'd entered his life, he'd tried to keep his distance. He didn't deserve her purity, goodness, or light. But dammit, he wanted it, anyway. And now his fucked-up past was going to cost him the best thing to ever happen to him. And he couldn't blame her for leaving.

Samantha was his sweet, guileless cupcake, a lightweight in every way. He'd known from the beginning that their lives were too vastly different, that someone like her wasn't cut out to live in his darkness long term.

By leaving, she was making everything easier, right? She would be safer at her parents' mansion than she ever would be with him, and he could deal with Wyatt without worrying about Samantha's safety. But knowing that didn't stop his heart from splintering in two.

"Okay. Do what you have to, but I don't want you leaving without some kind of security until the issue with Wyatt is resolved," he said, his voice sounding like he'd just swallowed glass.

She tipped her head, her silky hair keeping her face concealed from his view. "I called my father, and he's sending over a private car with his personal security. He should be here any minute," she said in a tight voice as she swiped her fingers beneath her eyes in a way that led him to believe she was clearing away tears.

At least she was affected somehow. He couldn't handle it if his was the only heart cracking into pieces. Then her words suddenly hit him.

*She'd called her father.*

Clay's worst nightmare had just come true, the one thing he'd fought like hell to help her prevent. She was going back to her parents and, ultimately, back to Harrison. She was going to marry a man she didn't love for the sake of her father's business—and give up her own identity in the process. That revelation had the worst kind of agony clawing through his stomach. But as much as he wanted to beg her to stay, he didn't have the right. He never had.

Just as she finished packing, a knock sounded on the apartment door, and Clay's heart slammed hard in his chest because he knew *this was it*. In another few minutes, she'd be gone, as if she'd never turned his life and emotions upside down and inside out.

She turned and met his gaze, her eyes filled with moisture and the same kind of dread that sat in his gut, holding him hostage.

"I have to go," she whispered in an aching voice.

"I know," he said, and did the only thing he could. He walked her to the door and delivered her to the man who'd come to take her home.

# Chapter Fourteen

IT HAD ONLY been one day without Samantha, but it already felt like a lifetime to Clay. Nothing was the same without her. Not his apartment. Not the bar. And especially not his empty bed. He'd gotten so used to having her around and in his life—seeing her smile, hearing her laugh, and smelling the sweet scent of whatever she'd decided to bake for the day. For the rest of his life, he knew that *nothing* would ever fill the cavernous hole inside of him that losing Samantha had left behind.

He loved her, and his main regret was that he'd never told her. But keeping that declaration buried deep inside of him had been the right thing to do. She was back home and safe from Wyatt, though Clay tried not to think about the fact that she'd most likely give in to her father's demands to marry Harrison. *Fuck.* That thought alone, and knowing that any other man had the right to touch her, made him crazy.

"Jesus Christ, Clay," Levi said, frowning at him from his seat across the bar, a hint of compassion in his brother's gaze. "I know that Samantha leaving has thrown you for a loop, but I need you to pay attention to what I'm about to tell you."

Thrown him for a loop? Hell, he'd been walking around in a fog, like a Goddamn lost puppy, emotionally shredded and lost without her. And everyone was treating him with kid gloves, including both of his brothers. There was nothing he could do to change the decision that Samantha had made, and in fairness to her, he hadn't even tried. So he forced his mind to clear so he could concentrate on the important information that Levi was here to share with him.

"I'm good," he said assured Levi gruffly, bracing his arms on the surface of the bar. "What did you find on Wyatt?" Clay wanted the prick out of their lives as quickly as possible, and hopefully for good this time.

"A lot of expected shit," Levi told him. "His criminal history is long and quite notable, with a few convictions, but his time served has been minimal."

Clay swore beneath his breath. "Is there no fucking justice in this world?"

"Actually, there is." A triumphant smile curved Levi's lips, as if he'd been holding back the best part. "While running his prints through the system, there was a match. He has a warrant out for his arrest."

Clay couldn't deny the anticipation that surged through him. "For?"

"First-degree murder."

A sick feeling of triumph shot through Clay, knowing that just maybe the monster would finally get what he deserved. "What did he do?"

"It was about a year ago. He was living with a woman who'd been arrested numerous times for drug possession and solicitation," Levi said, bringing back memories of their own mother's addictions and how Wyatt had taken advantage of her weakness, which was apparently the asshole's MO. "According to the files and records, his DNA was all over the crime scene, but they couldn't find him. He must have been lying low all this time. Like, *underground* low, because he's managed to avoid being caught and arrested."

"Yet he's surfaced now, asking for money. He must owe someone he's more afraid of than prison time," Clay mused. "So where does that leave us?"

"I talked to the detective on the case, told him the situation, and they're already in the process of setting up a sting to take him into custody whenever and wherever he tells you to meet him."

"What about the exchange of money?" First thing this morning, Clay had called his banker to set the withdrawal of cash in motion, but since it was such a large amount, he wouldn't be able to pick it up until the end of the day.

Levi shook his head. "The chief of police doesn't want a civilian involved in the takedown. They obviously want to keep any casualties to a minimum. Trust me, we don't need the blackmail and extortion charges to put this guy away. There is more than enough evidence to convict Wyatt, and murder is a capital charge, which means life without parole. He's going to rot in prison."

Clay exhaled a deep breath, releasing it slowly. He couldn't deny the relief he felt at knowing that *finally* justice would be served. But he wouldn't truly be able to relax until the fucker was behind bars, where he belonged.

"All you need to do is let me know the time and place as soon as you hear from Wyatt, and the PD will take care of everything else."

"Chances are he's going to show up here," Clay muttered.

"Then tell him you have to pick up the cash and will meet him somewhere neutral. Then call me with the details." Levi pinned him with a direct look, a distinct warning in his gaze. "Once that's done, you need to keep your ass here until we confirm we have Wyatt in custody, got it?"

"Got it." Clay wasn't going to do anything to jeopardize Wyatt's arrest.

"Good," Levi said, then pushed back his chair to stand and grinned. "Then my work here is done."

Clay walked his brother to the front entrance, let him out, then locked up after him since the bar didn't open for another two hours. He was halfway to his office when he heard a loud knock. Assuming Levi forgot to tell him something important, he returned and pulled the door open.

He was surprised to find a young, well-dressed man standing on the other side, appearing extremely nervous, his gaze darting up and down the deserted street. The guy looked as if he was making sure he wasn't about to get mugged. He clearly wasn't a Kincaid's regular. Everything about him was neat and orderly and wealthy-looking, from his short, styled hair to his immaculately pressed gray suit, all the way down to his polished leather shoes.

He was obviously on the *wrong* side of town, and even though Clay didn't discriminate, the bar was closed. "Sorry, but the place doesn't open until four," he told the other guy.

The man gave another surreptitious look around—which Clay found extremely amusing—before meeting Clay's gaze. "Actually, I'm here to speak with Clay Kincaid."

*Huh.* "That would be me," he said, crossing his arms over his chest.

The guy shifted uncomfortably on his feet. "Do you mind if I come in for a few minutes?"

Clay couldn't imagine what kind of business this dude had with him, but he noticed that he was carrying a thick manila envelope, and Clay was curious to know what he wanted. "Yeah, sure."

He stepped aside to let him in, then led the way into the main area, not missing the way the man's gaze took in the well-used bar, not so much in distaste but, rather, with a surprising amount of interest.

"So, what can I do for you, Mr...." Clay deliberately let the words trail off, which prompted an introduction.

"Blackwell," the guy said, though he didn't offer his hand to shake. "Harrison Blackwell."

Shock rendered Clay speechless as he stared at the other man—the perfect, wealthy, well-bred man who would most likely marry the woman *Clay* loved. He felt as though he'd been sucker-punched in the stomach and swallowed back an anguished groan.

A wry smile touched the corner of Harrison's mouth. "So, Samantha told you about me," he said, though there was no animosity or ill will in the other man's tone, just an odd acceptance that Clay didn't quite understand.

"She did." And if Harrison was here now, then that meant Samantha must have told the other guy about *him*, and Clay wasn't sure what to think about that. "What can I do for you?"

"I'm here to deliver a package." Harrison lifted the fat envelope he was holding, though he didn't hand it over just yet. "And I wanted to meet the man who Samantha gave up her new, independent life for."

Clay frowned in confusion. "Excuse me?" *What the fuck was the guy talking about?*

Harrison laughed and shook his head. "She didn't tell you, did she?"

"Tell me *what?*" he demanded irritably, damn close to shaking the words out of the man.

"She returned home in exchange for fifty thousand dollars delivered directly to you, in cash."

*Because she believed he needed the money to pay off Wyatt,* Clay realized. "And what strings were included in the exchange?" he asked impatiently through gritted teeth. Because Clay knew, without a doubt, her father had demanded blood in return.

"Samantha called her father yesterday and told him she needed money immediately, that you were in trouble and she wanted to help," Harrison said, looking him in the eye as he set the padded envelope of money on the table next to where they were standing. "And Conrad Jamieson, as you already surmised, struck a bargain with his own daughter. Her return home and agreement to marry me, in exchange for giving you fifty grand."

What. The. Hell? *Her father had bribed and blackmailed her.*

Clay felt so dizzy he nearly dropped to his knees as another realization struck him. Samantha hadn't gone back home because she was scared and no longer wanted to be with him. No, she'd sold her soul to her father to make sure Clay had the money to pay Wyatt. She'd done it *for* him, selflessly walking away from this new life she'd painstakingly created for herself, and giving up her dream of being a pastry chef, in order to ensure *he* was safe and protected.

How could he have been so blind not to have seen her actions for himself?

Harrison must have recognized Clay's stunned expression because he continued on, his tone softer. "The thing is, we've known all along where Samantha has been. The night she left, Conrad called the security firm he keeps on retainer and made sure they found out exactly where she was. They updated Conrad with daily reports, and when she ended up staying here with you, he was provided with a full background report on you, as well."

Clay instinctively cringed, certain a man like Conrad Jamieson hadn't been happy to discover Clay's past. No doubt the other man felt Clay wasn't good enough for his daughter. Yet he'd left Samantha alone for three weeks, *with him*. "If Conrad knew where Samantha was, why didn't he just come and get her?"

Harrison shrugged. "There was something in your background report that assured him that you were trustworthy, so he figured that Samantha just needed to sow some wild oats before she settled down and married me."

"For the sake of the investment firm."

"That would be correct," Harrison said with an impassive nod. "I know Samantha doesn't love me, and quite frankly, I don't love her, either. She's too spirited, way too independent, and I know she'd be miserable in a structured marriage like ours would be. She wants to have her own life, her own career, and the fact that she gave it all up and agreed to her father's terms, in exchange for this money, tells me just how important you are to her."

It was as if Harrison was giving him permission to go after Samantha, and maybe, the other man would be grateful for not having to go through with the arranged marriage, too.

"Why are you telling me this?" Clay asked.

"Because despite everything, I'd rather see Samantha living the kind of life she wants to, with the one person who will support her and make her happy," Harrison said, his voice ringing with sincerity. "And I know that man is not me."

Fuck yeah, because *Clay was that man*. And he'd do whatever it took to fight for Samantha, to make sure she knew she was his in every way and belonged right here, with him.

"Have a good afternoon, Mr. Kincaid," Harrison said, then turned around and walked back toward the entrance.

Once Clay heard the door shut, he sat down in the nearest chair, his heart pounding so hard in his chest it was like a roar in his ears. He caught sight of the envelope of cash that Harrison had left behind, once again in awe of what Samantha was willing to sacrifice for him.

The ironic thing was, he didn't need the money. Hell, he had more than enough in the bank to pay off Wyatt—not that Clay needed to do that any longer—and for them to buy a real house and furnish it any way she wanted. Yeah, he was jumping ahead of himself, but he couldn't help it. He wanted everything with Samantha, and he wanted it *now*.

Clay's first instinct was to take the money to Conrad Jamieson and bring Samantha back where she belonged. But he couldn't, not just yet. Not until he knew for certain that Wyatt was off the streets and there was no threat to Samantha's safety.

But once that happened, he was going to get his girl.

✧   ✧   ✧

CLAY SPENT THE next day pacing in his apartment like a caged animal, anxious and edgy as he impatiently waited for Levi's call that Wyatt was in custody. Hours passed, and just when Clay thought he was going to climb the walls, his brother *finally* contacted him. The sting had gone off without a hitch.

While Wyatt had initially taken off running when he realized he'd been set up, he'd been surrounded by a dozen undercover cops who apprehended him before he could get away and charged him with first-degree murder. The best part? Levi had been the one to look the prick in the eyes as he read Wyatt his Miranda rights.

As soon as Clay disconnected the call with Levi, he picked up the envelope of cash on the table, along with his car keys, and headed out to his truck. Levi, being the awesome brother that he was, had given him the address to the Jamieson estate in River Forest, and Clay headed in that direction, not caring that he was driving over the speed limit. He'd risk a ticket for Samantha. Hell, he'd risk *anything* to be with her.

When Clay arrived at the address, he reached his first roadblock. The house was secured by a massive gate that required him to press an intercom and announce himself. It made sense that someone as wealthy and high-profile as Conrad Jamieson would have an elaborate security system, and Clay reluctantly gave his name to the person on the other side of the speaker and told them that he was there to see Conrad. Once Clay settled things with Samantha's father, he'd head straight for her.

The intercom went silent, and, filled with dread, Clay waited for some kind of reply. For a long moment, he thought he was going to be denied entry, but finally those huge iron barriers parted to let him in. And it was damn good thing, too, because Clay was not opposed to scaling the fence in order to get to the house and Samantha.

The driveway leading up to the enormous house was long, ending in a circular drive in front of the mansion. He parked his truck, and, envelope in hand, he got out of the vehicle and rang the doorbell. Seconds later, a middle-aged woman dressed in a crisp white shirt and black slacks greeted him and politely requested he follow her to Conrad's study.

The old man was obviously waiting for him.

The inside of the house looked like a palace. Hell, it *was* a palace compared to anyplace he'd ever lived— shockingly ostentatious and an obvious showcase for all the wealth that Conrad had amassed. And it was so not reflective of the woman he'd come to know over the past three weeks. No, Samantha had been sweet and unpretentious, and completely at ease without all this opulence and grandeur.

It felt as though they'd walked a mile before the housemaid finally stopped in front of a set of closed double doors and turned to him with a smile. "Mr. Jamieson is waiting for you inside," she said, then left him standing alone.

He put his hand on the decorative gold doorknob and exhaled a deep breath. He'd thought he'd at least be intimidated about meeting Samantha's father for the first time, especially under the current circumstances, but Clay was so certain of his feelings for the man's daughter that any anxiety took a backseat to his intentions—if that's what she wanted, too. Because he realized that for all his self-assurance, the two of them had never talked about being *together* beyond the temporary affair they'd agreed to.

*Yeah, that's because you were a grade-A idiot who clammed up anytime things got too emotional between you.*

All that was about to change.

Shoulders back and head held high, he opened the door and stepped inside yet another lavishly decorated room that smelled like leather and some kind of exotic spice. Samantha's father sat behind an enormous desk in an equally imposing chair that—no doubt deliberately—made him look like a king sitting on his throne.

*Let the beheading commence*, Clay thought with wry humor as he walked the rest of the way inside the study.

Conrad leaned back in his chair, deceptively casual as he watched Clay's approach.

Clay wasn't afraid of the older man, but he'd be a liar if he didn't admit that it would be nice to have his approval. However, gaining Samantha's parents' blessing wasn't a requirement for him to lay his heart out and give her the choice of being with him forever.

He stopped in front of the desk. "Mr. Jamieson," Clay acknowledged with a nod, determined to treat the man with respect, despite the fact that he'd blackmailed his daughter into staying away from Clay.

He then pushed the envelope of cash across the surface, well aware of the other man scrutinizing everything about him. "While I appreciate the money you sent to help me out, I'm returning it all. I don't want it. I don't need it. In fact, you had to have known that I've got a couple million dollars sitting in the bank, since you did a background check on me. So why even bother?" Clay asked the question that had been swirling in his head ever since Harrison had left the bar.

"Two reasons, actually," the older man said evenly. "One, it worked to bring Samantha back home. And two, I wanted to know what kind of man you truly are."

*So it had been some kind of test?* Clay kept hold of his temper, reminding himself that testing Clay was the man's way of looking out for his child—as screwed up as that might be.

"To be honest with you, sir, I'm more than a little pissed to find out the money came with an ultimatum to Samantha."

The corner of Conrad's mouth twitched with something akin to amusement before he shrugged, his expression once again bland. "I was getting tired of waiting for my daughter to come to her senses and come home."

"So you blackmailed her?" Clay swallowed back the bitterness threatening to surface. "You forced her to give up the life *she* wanted so you could use her as some kind of collateral to secure your business and marry her off to a man she doesn't love?"

A spark of anger flickered in Conrad's gaze. "She's my child, and I want the best for her."

"Then let her make her own decisions." Clay braced his hands on the edge of Conrad's desk and leaned closer, his impatience getting the best of him. "Let her live her own life."

Conrad frowned at Clay. "That's difficult for a man like me to do."

A man who wanted complete control over everyone and everything in his domain.

Clay straightened again, aware he was fighting for both Samantha and the life she wanted to live. "It's not about what *you* want. You can't force a vibrant, independent woman like Samantha to be someone or something she isn't and expect her to be happy." Though he wondered if Samantha's happiness mattered in the scheme of Conrad's needs and plans.

Rocking back in his chair, the older man eyed Clay speculatively. "And where do *you* think you fit into my daughter's life?"

"Same answer, sir. It isn't about what I want, either. But I do know I will do everything in my power to make her happy."

"Happiness in the way you mean it is way overrated." Conrad raised a brow. "You do realize you're all wrong for her."

Clay felt as though the old man was testing him again, otherwise he'd have thrown him out by now. Although he didn't appreciate the hoops he had to jump through, this man, whether he liked him or not, was Samantha's father.

And Clay loved Samantha. "I may not be an investment banker or someone from your social circle, but I've never felt anything as *right* as being with Samantha."

"And you're certain she feels the same way?" Conrad asked.

Clay thought of their last night together and knew it with absolute certainty. "Yes, I am."

"Let me tell you something, son," Conrad said, his tone surprisingly calm as he met Clay's gaze. "I didn't like what I read in your background report, and your past leaves *a lot* to be desired. But the man you've become despite how you grew up is what impresses me." He steepled his fingers and studied Clay through a narrow but, dare he say, *approving* gaze? "I admire the fact that you overcame such adversity, that you raised your brothers, and that you help people less fortunate."

Clay swallowed hard, shocked as hell that the other

man was giving him even that much validation. And despite telling himself that what other people thought didn't matter, he was surprised to find that what Samantha's father thought of him did. At least a little.

Sensing Conrad wasn't finished, Clay remained silent.

"Ultimately, you took care of Samantha when a lesser man would have taken advantage of her, especially after finding out who she is and what she's worth."

Clay shook his head in annoyance. "None of that matters to me." He tapped the envelope on the desk, reinforcing his point.

"I believe you. And that's exactly what I was hoping you'd do."

Clay shook his head, not surprised he'd been right. The money had been a test. He held on to his anger, reminding himself Conrad Jamieson lived in a world Clay couldn't even begin to fathom.

"If I had my choice, Samantha would marry Harrison," Conrad said flat out, not sugarcoating his feelings. "I told myself what she had with you was just a little fling, and she'd get bored and tired of doing *without*. That she'd come back home, settle down, and appreciate the fact that marrying Harrison would provide her with the lifestyle she was accustomed to, and the firm would remain in the family."

Clay clenched his jaw, disgusted by the man's lack of faith in his daughter's self-worth and independence.

"Needless to say, when she called me and told me

that she needed the money, I saw my chance to make sure she returned home where she belongs and left you behind." Conrad exhaled, the sound rife with resignation. "But here you are, returning the money, which tells me much about your character and even more about what my daughter means to you."

Clay remained in place, but this conversation was taking too long, when all he wanted to do was get to Samantha. Still, he would give the man the respect he didn't deserve. For a few more minutes max, then he was going after his woman.

"For what it's worth, about an hour ago, Samantha informed me and her mother that despite the fact that we'd helped you out, she was going back to you tonight. My daughter is determined to be with you even if she has to work every day of her life to pay us back." He shook his head. "Like I need the God-damned money."

Clay couldn't stop the grin that tugged at his lips. Yeah, that was his sassy cupcake.

Conrad managed a reluctant laugh, too. "She's defiant and stubborn, and I really tried to give her the best. But what I'm coming to realize is that I could never force Samantha to fit into the mold that her mother and I so painstakingly groomed her for. Not without her coming to resent us more than she already does."

"She's independent and proud. Like you," Clay said.

Conrad let out a heavy sigh. "Letting her go is one

of the most difficult things we've ever done, but I don't want to lose my only child, and that's what would happen if I did anything more to keep her away from you."

Clay could only imagine how difficult this was for a dignified man like Conrad to admit. But it was clear that he truly loved his daughter, and when push came to shove, he wasn't going to coerce her to stay and marry a man she didn't love. Clay gave him props for that.

So he did what he could to assure him that Samantha would always be in good hands. "I know I'm not who you would have hand-picked for her, but I can promise you that I will do everything in my power to give her a good life. To protect her and respect her and be the kind of man who deserves a woman as special as she is."

"Since I have no choice in the matter, that's what I'm counting on," Conrad said gruffly.

"I love your daughter," Clay said, just in case his feelings mattered. They were words he'd never spoken to another woman before, and he realized he'd been waiting all his life for the *right* woman. For Samantha.

Clay heard a soft gasp from behind him, and he turned around to find Samantha standing in the doorway, her eyes wide and shimmering with moisture as she stared at him in surprise. His heart thumped painfully hard in his chest. She was so damn beautiful, and nothing else in the world mattered except making her his.

"Do you mean it?" she asked, her voice quivering with emotion.

He cleared the tightness from his own throat and smiled. *Yes, he absolutely loved her.* "Cupcake, you should know by now that I always mean what I say. I love you, more than I thought I could ever love another person. And I don't want to live another day without you in it. Ever."

Unable to stand the distance between them, he started for her at the same time she ran toward him. When she reached Clay, she jumped into his arms, securing her arms around his neck and wrapping her legs around his waist. He laughed at her enthusiasm and anchored his arms under her butt to hold her in place as she buried her face against his neck, holding him so impossibly tight.

"I love you so much, Clay." She pressed her hands to his jaw and looked into his eyes. "There is no way I could have stayed away from you."

"Me, either," he said, meaning it.

Her father cleared his throat, and Samantha surprised Clay with a laugh. "Get used to it, Daddy." Grinning, she stroked her thumbs across Clay's cheeks, her gaze suddenly filled with regret. "The moment I got home, I realized what a huge mistake I made. I'm so sorry."

"Just don't ever leave me again."

"Never," she promised, then said the words he wanted to hear. "Take me home."

✧   ✧   ✧

AS SOON AS they reached Kincaid's, Clay lifted Samantha out of his truck and hauled her over his shoulder like a caveman claiming his woman. And that's exactly how he felt, and *claiming her* was definitely first on the agenda.

Hanging upside down with his arms banded around her knees to keep her in place, she laughed happily as he carried her across the parking lot and up the back stairs, then into his apartment.

The moment he stepped through the threshold and the door was closed behind them, he smacked her on the ass through the cute little dress she was wearing, sharp enough for her to suck in a startled breath.

"Owww!" she protested as she squirmed on his shoulder. "What was that for?"

"*That* was for not telling me why you were leaving me." He swatted her again, more lightly this time. "And that was for not letting me know you planned to ask your father for the money to bail me out of trouble," he said as he continued on his way into the bedroom.

"But you needed it," she insisted. "For Wyatt."

He flipped her onto the bed, flat on her back. He straddled her thighs, and she looked up at him with that soft, hot look of desire in her gaze. But he refused to be distracted until they settled a few things.

"Let's get one very important thing straight right now," he said, bracing his hands beside her head so they were face-to-face. "I don't need your money, your parents' money, or anyone else's money. I have a couple million sitting in an investment account that I inherited from Jerry with this bar."

Her dark blue eyes grew round with shock. "But you told Wyatt you didn't have the money!"

"Of course I told him that," he said, and rolled his eyes. "I wasn't just going to hand the cash over to him."

Her expression suddenly turned serious with concern as she pressed her hands on his chest. "Did *you* pay him the money then?"

"No." He gave her the abbreviated version for now, because the talking was killing the moment and he was *dying* to get inside of her. "Levi did some digging and discovered there was a warrant for Wyatt's arrest. They took him into custody this afternoon and charged him with first-degree murder. He'll be put away for the rest of his life."

She exhaled a relieved breath. "Thank God. I couldn't bear the thought of something happening to you."

He grinned wickedly as he reached down to the hem of her dress and pulled it up and over her head. "Nothing is going to happen to me, Cupcake…except for some hot, dirty sex."

He touched her between her thighs, sliding his hand over her damp flesh, and that's all it took for her *talking* to turn into delightful moans of pleasure. The kind he intended to surround himself with for the rest of their lives.

# Epilogue

*Six months later...*

SAMANTHA FINISHED UP her afternoon shift at Adeline's a bit early, excitement and nerves swarming inside her as she got into the cute MINI Cooper that Clay had bought for her. She headed over to Inked, planning to do something wild, crazy, and naughty. Something that would drive Clay mad, in a very good way.

She stepped into the tattoo shop and met Katrina at the front counter.

"Are you absolutely sure you want to do this?" her friend asked before showing Samantha the design she'd created for her. "Once it's done, it's permanent, unless you want to go through painful laser removal treatments."

As soon as she saw the small hand-drawn image,

she felt giddy with excitement. "I'm absolutely sure. I've been wanting to do this for months." Her very first tattoo, and it was a surprise for Clay.

"You have become such a bad girl," Katrina teased.

"I know," Samantha said with a carefree laugh. "I love being bad."

Katrina grinned. "Come on, follow me back to Mason's cubicle, and we'll get you started."

When Katrina reached the private area, she rapped on the partition to get his attention before stepping inside. "Your appointment is here."

Mason glanced up, shock transforming his dark, gorgeous features when his gaze fell on Samantha. "What the hell?"

Samantha raised a brow at Katrina. "You didn't tell him it was me?"

She shook her head and grinned. "He would have said no. The element of surprise is much better."

Mason frowned at both of them before pinning Samantha with a severe look. "I'm not touching you. You're a fucking virgin."

Samantha unbuttoned her light pink pastry chef coat and hung it up on a nearby hook for jackets and sweaters, which left her just wearing a camisole. "Trust me, after being with your brother for six months, I'm no virgin, so no worries there," she said playfully.

"Ugh." Mason cringed. "I do *not* need to hear about my brother's dirty, kinky sex life."

"Why not?" Samantha replied in a lighthearted

tone. "We've been exposed to yours often enough."

"Whatever," he muttered, though he didn't deny the truth of his man-whoring ways. "Does Clay know?"

Samantha shook her head. "It's a surprise."

Mason muttered a curse. "He is going to kick my ass."

"Not my problem," she said sweetly, waiting for someone to tell her what she needed to do to get this party started. But Mason was sitting on his little stool, still not looking at all pleased with the situation.

Katrina sighed impatiently at Mason. "Since you suddenly seem to have an issue with virgins, would you rather Cain do her? This tattoo is going right below the bikini line."

"Hell no. No one else is going to *do her* but me," Mason growled irritably as he grabbed the small transfer paper with the design Katrina had come up with. "Lie down before I change my mind."

Samantha reclined on the padded leather table while Mason prepared his station. Since she wanted the image near her hipbone but below the waistband of her panties, she had to lift her camisole up a few inches, unbutton her pants, and pull them down a bit, too.

Mason helped her, his touch professional while keeping her decent at all times. After washing his hands and putting on sterile gloves, he cleaned the area with a spray of alcohol, then rubbed on a smear of gel that allowed the transfer to adhere to her skin. He applied the image, gave her a mirror to confirm the placement, then uncapped a few colors of bright ink.

"My brother is going to fucking chop off my balls for touching you, let alone putting ink on your body," Mason muttered.

"You let me handle Clay," she said, knowing that he was going to love the tattoo once he saw it.

Mason glanced at her as he picked up his tattoo machine, his gaze meeting hers. "He's really happy, you know," he said, suddenly serious, a hint of gratitude in his eyes. "Happier than I've ever seen him. Because of you."

She smiled. "I'm glad. He makes me happy, too." That was an understatement. Clay made her feel whole and complete. He enriched her life in so many ways, making her feel loved and protected and sexy—every single day.

Mason frowned as he returned his focus to the design, clearly hesitant to mar her *virgin* skin. After a moment, he settled his hands across her abdomen and positioned the needle right above the design. "Okay, close your eyes, try to relax, and just breathe through the pain. This is small, so it shouldn't take long."

The sudden buzz of the tattoo gun startled her, and when the needle touched her skin, she wanted to scream at the intense scraping sensation making her flesh burn like fire. Holy shit, how in the world did people get more than one tattoo? Let alone cover their bodies, like Katrina with her full sleeve of colorful butterflies? Samantha prayed she survived her first one!

Mason chuckled. "No turning back now, sweetheart. Keep breathing and go to your happy place."

And that's what Samantha did. She inhaled and exhaled, slow and deep, and let her mind wander, which usually took her one of two places—to thoughts of Clay or thoughts of some kind of new pastry she wanted to bake. Those were the two most important things in her life, and she never wanted one without the other.

Since the day Clay had come to her parents' house and whisked her away, her life had become fun, exciting, and everything she'd dreamed it could be. Adeline had hired her right after her interview, and while she'd initially started out as just a baker, over the past few months, she'd proven herself and had been promoted to pastry chef. She baked all sorts of desserts for businesses and catering halls while also handling the front-end bakery that sold to the public.

Her career, along with her life with Clay, and being with him every day and night, was pretty damn perfect.

She was still working on mending her relationship with her parents. Even though they'd reluctantly accepted her decision to be with Clay, it had taken a while for the tension between them to ebb to the point that they were finally comfortable around each other again.

She and Clay had gone to the house for a few Sunday brunches, and she could tell that her father was gradually warming up to Clay. The last time they'd visited, her dad had jokingly asked Clay how he felt about working in the corporate world, to which Clay had replied with an honest *hell no*, making it very clear that he had no interest whatsoever in the investment firm.

She'd just gotten used to the pain of the needle—either that or her skin had gone numb—when Mason turned off his machine and announced that they were done. He gave her the hand mirror to check out her new ink.

She grinned when she saw what a great job Mason had done on the tattoo. It looked exactly like a cupcake, with a swirl of fluffy pink frosting and multicolored heart sprinkles on top. Across the bottom was a small banner that said *Life is Sweet* in a pretty cursive font.

She couldn't wait to show Clay and knew what that peek of her tattoo would lead to—getting naked and a whole lot of other sexy fun. She was counting on it.

Mason wiped a small amount of ointment on her skin and covered the new ink with a patch of saran wrap to protect it for the first twenty-four hours. He gave her a sheet of aftercare instructions, and after showing off her new ink to Katrina, she headed home.

When she arrived in the apartment, Clay was in the kitchen getting something to drink, waiting for her to get home from work as he did every day—instead of spending all his time down at the bar. Bursting with enthusiasm and her little secret, she approached him, and without hesitating, she kissed him, hot and deep.

She moaned in pure contentment when he took

over, tangling his tongue with hers, his mouth so hungry, so greedy. She couldn't get enough of him. Never would. She moved against him, and with a deep growl, he wrapped a strong arm around her back and pulled her so tight against him she could feel every hard muscle, including the one thickening in his pants. *Umm, yeah.*

Too soon, he ended the kiss and buried his face against her neck, inhaling her scent and licking the column of her throat with his tongue. "You come home every day from work smelling like a delicious cupcake," he said as he slid his hands down to cup her ass and squeeze each cheek. "I just want to eat you up before fucking you senseless."

She laughed, the sound husky and one hundred percent aroused. "Yes, please."

In the next instant, she was swept up into his arms as he carried her into the bedroom, holding her as if she were as light as a feather, which she knew she wasn't.

She smiled up at him. "I have a surprise for you."

"Yeah?" He looked interested, but once Clay's mind was on sex, it was hard to deter him. "Can it wait until after I'm done eating my cupcake?"

He dropped her on the bed and didn't wait for an answer as he pulled off her camisole—which conveniently came with a built-in bra—then removed her shoes and socks and helped her shimmy out of her pants. When he reached for her panties, that's when he finally saw the edge of the plastic wrap protecting her new ink.

His gaze flew up to hers. "Holy shit. You got a tattoo."

"A *real* one," she teased, just in case he thought it was one of those temporary deals.

With a worried frown, he inched down the waistband of her underwear until he could see the design.

"Surprise," she said impishly. "A cupcake. Just for you."

A huge grin spread across his face, which was exactly what she wanted to see. But it didn't last long as his brows suddenly furrowed together. "Who did the tattoo?"

She bit her bottom lip. "Umm, Mason."

"*Here?*" he said incredulously. "Right near your—"

Laughing, she covered his mouth with her palm before he could say the word *pussy*, but he pulled her hand away.

"I'm going to fucking kill him," he growled.

She rolled her eyes. "Trust me, he didn't *want* to do it, because he was afraid you were going to chop off his balls," she said with a laugh. "Would you rather have had some strange guy do the work?"

"No," he said sullenly, which gradually gave way to a lascivious look as he pulled her panties off the rest of the way and quickly stripped off his own clothes. "Let's put you on top so I don't crush your cupcake," he said as he moved onto the bed beside her. He stretched out on his back, then pulled her on top of his body so that she was straddling his hips, his shaft poised right between her legs.

There was no need for a condom anymore. They

were exclusive, she was on the pill, and they'd both been tested. He rubbed the tip of his cock through her already wet, slick folds, then pushed the head just inside of her. Grabbing her waist in his hands, he pulled her down the same time he thrust up inside her.

Samantha gasped, her body shuddering as he filled her. And then she looked down at him, ensnared in his heated gaze, and began to move. Bracing her hands on his abdomen, she rode him, slow and deep.

It didn't take them long to find a mutual release, and when they were both spent, she collapsed on top of Clay until they could breath normally again. He stroked her hair and along her back, and she was too content to move off of him.

"I have a surprise for you, too," he said after a while.

"Yeah?" She lifted her head so she could look at his face. "What is it? Did you get a tattoo, too? One that says Saint Clay?" she teased.

"Smartass." He smacked her bare bottom, making her yelp, but they were both smiling and relaxed. "I contacted a Realtor. I think it's time we looked for a real house to live in."

She blinked in surprise. "I like living here."

"I know you do," he said softly as he tucked a stray strand of hair behind her ear. "But I plan to marry you, and this place doesn't give us much room to grow."

Her heart sped up, and she swallowed hard. "Are you *asking* me to marry you?"

"Yeah, I guess I am," he said, his voice gruff with

emotion and his eyes flickering with anticipation as his hands gently framed her face. "Will you marry me, Cupcake? I don't want to live a single day without you. You've changed my life and made me a better man. And most importantly, I love you, and I need to know you're mine. Forever."

Tears of pure joy filled her eyes. This amazing man had come so far since the night they'd met, but what he didn't realize was that he'd changed her life, as well. They were good together, and good for each other.

She nodded much too eagerly and didn't even care. "Yes, I'll marry you. As soon as possible."

He laughed, looking happy and pleased. "How do you feel about a small Vegas wedding?"

Her parents would want a formal ceremony and big reception, but she'd never subject Clay to that. She didn't want or need the fanfare, either, so her decision was an easy one.

"I think a Vegas wedding sounds perfect," she murmured.

He groaned in contentment, then rolled her off him and glanced at her new tattoo again, careful not to remove the wrapping. "I can't wait to touch it and lick it and swirl my tongue over that frosting," he murmured wickedly.

"I can't wait, either," she said, knowing she'd be his cupcake for the rest of their lives.

Next up: Mason Kincaid –
Get **DIRTY SEXY INKED** Today!

Thank you for reading DIRTY SEXY SAINT. We would appreciate it if you would help others enjoy this book too. Please recommend to others and leave a review.

Sign up for Carly Phillips & Erika Wilde's Newsletters:

Carly's Newsletter
http://smarturl.it/CarlysNewsletter

Erika's Newsletter
http://smarturl.it/ErikaWildeNewsletter

Dirty Sexy Series Reading Order:
Dirty Sexy Saint (Clay Kincaid)
Dirty Sexy Inked (Mason Kincaid)
Dirty Sexy Cuffed (Levi Kincaid)
*Every book in the Dirty Sexy series can be read alone for your reading enjoyment!

Read on for Excerpts of Carly & Erika's books:
Dare to Love by Carly Phillips
The Awakening (The Marriage Diaries, Vol. 1) by
    Erika Wilde

## Dare to Love

## Excerpt

### by Carly Phillips

Once a year, the Dare siblings gathered at the Club Meridian Ballroom in South Florida to celebrate the birthday of the father many of them despised. Ian Dare raised his glass filled with Glenlivet and took a sip, letting the slow burn of fine scotch work its way down his throat and into his system. He'd need another before he fully relaxed.

"Hi, big brother." His sister Olivia strode up to him and nudged him with her elbow.

"Watch the drink," he said, wrapping his free arm around her shoulders for an affectionate hug. "Hi, Olivia."

She returned the gesture with a quick kiss on his cheek. "It's nice of you to be here."

He shrugged. "I'm here for Avery and for you. Although why you two forgave him—"

"Uh-uh. Not here." She wagged a finger in front of his face. "If I have to put on a dress, we're going to act civilized."

Ian stepped back and took in his twenty-four-year-old sister for the first time. Wearing a gold gown, her dark hair up in a chic twist, it was hard to believe she was the same bane of his existence who'd chased after him and his friends until they relented and let her play ball with them.

"You look gorgeous," he said to her.

She grinned. "You have to say that."

"I don't. And I mean it. I'll have to beat men off with sticks when they see you." The thought darkened his mood.

"You do and I'll have your housekeeper short-sheet your bed! Again, there should be perks to getting dressed like this, and getting laid should be one of them."

"I'll pretend I didn't hear that," he muttered and took another sip of his drink.

"You not only promised to come tonight, you swore you'd behave."

Ian scowled. "Good behavior ought to be optional considering the way he flaunts his assets," he said with a nod toward where Robert Dare held court.

Around him sat his second wife of nine years, Savannah Dare, and their daughter, Sienna, along with their nearest and dearest country club friends. Missing were their other two sons, but they'd show up soon.

Olivia placed a hand on his shoulder. "He loves her, you know. And Mom's made her peace."

"Mom had no choice once she found out about *her*."

Robert Dare had met the much younger Savannah

Sheppard and, to hear him tell it, fallen instantly in love. She was now the mother of his three other children, the oldest of whom was twenty-five. Ian had just turned thirty. Anyone could do the math and come up with two families at the same time. The man was beyond fertile, that was for damned sure.

At the reminder, Ian finished his drink and placed the tumbler on a passing server's tray. "I showed my face. I'm out of here." He started for the exit.

"Ian, hold on," his sister said, frustration in her tone.

"What? Do you want me to wait until they sing 'Happy Birthday'? No thanks. I'm leaving."

Before they could continue the discussion, their half brother Alex strode through the double entrance with a spectacular-looking woman holding tightly to his arm, and Ian's plans changed.

Because of *her*.

Some people had presence; others merely wished they possessed that magic something. In her bold, red dress and fuck-me heels, she owned the room. And he wanted to own her. Petite and curvy, with long, chocolate-brown hair that fell down her back in wild curls, she was the antithesis of every too-thin female he'd dated and kept at arm's length. But she was with his half brother, which meant he had to steer clear.

"I thought you were leaving," Olivia said from beside him.

"I am." He should. If he could tear his gaze away from *her*.

"If you wait for Tyler and Scott, you might just

relax enough to have fun," she said of their brothers. "Come on, please?" Olivia used the pleading tone he never could resist.

"Yeah, please, Ian? Come on," his sister Avery said, joining them, looking equally mature in a silver gown that showed way too much cleavage. At twenty-two, she was similar in coloring and looks to Olivia, and he wasn't any more ready to think of her as a grown-up—never mind letting other men ogle her—than he was with her sister.

Ian set his jaw, amazed these two hadn't been the death of him yet.

"So what am I begging him to do?" Avery asked Olivia.

Olivia grinned. "I want him to stay and hang out for a while. Having fun is probably out of the question, but I'm trying to persuade him to let loose."

"Brat," he muttered, unable to hold back a smile at Olivia's persistence.

He stole another glance at his lady in red. He could no more leave than he could approach her, he thought, frustrated because he was a man of action, and right now, he could do nothing but watch her.

"Well?" Olivia asked.

He forced his gaze to his sister and smiled. "Because you two asked so nicely, I'll stay." But his attention remained on the woman now dancing and laughing with his half brother.

Start Reading Dare to Love NOW!

# The Awakening

## Excerpt

*by Erika Wilde*

"**C**ome on, Jill, you can do it. It's not as though you've never seduced your husband before."

Sitting in her parked car, Jillian Noble exhaled a deep breath and waited for her encouraging pep talk to take effect and ease her nerves. Biting absently on her bottom lip, she stared up at the glass and chrome building where her husband's security consulting firm, Noble & Associates, resided on the twenty-eighth floor of the San Diego building. It was nearly two in the afternoon, and with Dean's silver Aston Martin Vantage coupe tucked neatly into his reserved spot, she knew he was in his office.

Now, it was just a matter of her gathering up the courage to saunter into Dean's domain and show her husband of nearly twenty years that she wanted to shake up their sex life.

At the age of thirty-eight, as well as being an ex-Navy SEAL who regularly trained with the men he hired to work for his security firm, Dean was still a gorgeous, virile man who enjoyed sex just as much as she did. But years of her focusing on raising their two sons along with being a wife and mother, and Dean working crazy long hours to ensure his security company was a success, well, the intimacy between them had become too predictable and routine. Somewhere along the way, they'd lost the intensity, the excitement and spontaneity, and she wanted all that back again... and much, much more.

Now that both boys were away—one in college and one enlisted in the Navy—and it was just her and Dean, she was ready to make the two of them a priority and revive their sex life in a major way, and take them both places they'd never dared to go before. Dark, erotic places she instinctively knew her husband had shied away from because he feared there was a part of his abusive father lurking deep inside him, and his biggest fear had always been that he'd go too far and hurt her.

With all her heart and soul, Jill knew her husband would never physically harm her, despite his own doubts. He'd never, ever, laid a hand on either of their two boys, not even when she, herself, wanted to strangle one of them for their idiotic teenage antics. Instead, Dean had taken the quiet and direct approach in disciplining their sons—starting with a strict discussion about right and wrong, and then he'd doled out their punishment, which usually included some kind of hard labor that gave them plenty of time to think about the stupidity of their actions.

Simple, but always effective.

A small smile curved the corner of her mouth. She'd be lying if she didn't admit that Dean could absolutely be over-bearing, possessive, and a bit controlling at times, but in their nineteen years of marriage, he'd never given her a reason not to trust him, in all ways.

Today would be the defining factor in their marriage. In the past, just as things got interesting in the bedroom, he'd pull back and gentle his touch and soften his words. The romance of making love had its place, but she wanted the raw, primitive man she knew Dean could be. And if it took a bit of coaxing to get him to release that staunch control of his and let go of all those fears holding him back, well, she figured she might as well have fun giving it her best shot.

Exhaling a deep breath, she stepped out of her Chevy Suburban and headed toward the building, her four inch black stilettos clicking on the paved walkway, then the marbled floors inside the lobby. Reaching the elevators, she stepped inside and punched the button for the twenty-eight floor.

On the flight up, she battled the nerves fluttering in her belly, the ones that made her question her sanity for going through with her outrageous plan. But then the double doors *whooshed* opened and Gail, the firm's long-time secretary, glanced up and greeted her with a genuine smile.

Now that Jill had been seen and recognized, there was no backing out now, so she walked into the plush reception area and stopped at the older woman's desk.

"Good afternoon, Jill," the other woman said, as warm and welcoming as always.

Jill smiled and tried to act casual, even though she was feeling anything but calm inside. "Hi, Gail. I'm here to see Dean. Is he available?"

"Absolutely. He's in his office." Gail reached for the phone on her desk. "Would you like for me to let him know you're here?"

"No, I'd rather surprise him," Jill said, stopping Gail before she could announce her presence and she lost the element of throwing her husband a little off kilter. Gaining the upper hand in any situation didn't happen often with Dean, and this was one time it would definitely work to her advantage.

"I'm sure he'd like that." Gail waved a hand toward the back offices, giving Jill the silent go-ahead.

She walked past Gail's desk, belatedly realizing just how close the secretary was to the other offices. Just behind the reception area was a large conference room, and she recognized the deep male voice talking as Dean's partner, Brent "Mac" MacMillan.

She glanced surreptitiously inside as she passed and saw the back of Mac's broad shoulders, and three other big, buff, good-looking men who worked security detail for the company. They were standing straight in a row with their feet braced apart and hands clasped behind their backs in a stance she recognized as military trained.

Because Mac commanded their attention as he issued instructions for their next security detail, none of the three men acknowledged her, though their intuitive gazes definitely tracked her progress as she strolled by. The men Dean and Mac hired were all ex-military—tough, bad-ass, alpha men like her husband. Silent, always aware, and incredibly intense. Only the absolute best of the best for Noble and Associates.

She continued on her way. To the right was Mac's currently empty office, and to the left was her husband's. His door was halfway closed, and she knocked on the wooden surface before slipping inside and making an appearance.

He glanced up from the paperwork he'd been perusing, his dark, sable brows still furrowed in concentration. As soon as he saw her, his gray eyes flickered with surprise, then quickly shifted to concern. Because she knew him so well, she caught the subtle tensing of his body, that vigilant awareness that something was off.

"Hey, baby," he said, his calm tone belying just how alert he was. "Is everything okay?"

"Everything is just fine," she rushed to reassure him, before his over-protective demeanor took over and derailed her plans. She understood his worry—she didn't stop by the office often, and never without calling him first. Of course he'd think the worst.

She closed the door and pressed in the lock to assure them privacy, which didn't escape his notice. Knowing the rest of her plan succeeding now relied on Dean's response to what she did next, she bolstered her confidence one last time and slowly strolled toward him.

She put an extra sway in her hips, and tugged loose the tie on her wrap-around dress. She allowed the fabric to flutter open in front, just enough to tantalize him with a smooth expanse of thigh as she walked. Predictably, his gaze immediately dropped to the flash of skin, and the last of her nerves gave way to anticipation.

"I want to get your opinion on something I bought today," she said huskily.

He never cared about what she purchased for herself, but then again, she rarely spent frivolously or excessively, even when he encouraged her to spoil herself. They were well-off now, his company worth millions, but when they'd first married right out of high school with a baby on the way, saving and budgeting had become a habit for her—one she was just learning to break every once in a while. After today, she hoped to have a reason to continue to splurge.

"I went to Sugar and Spice today to visit Raina, and I found something I thought you might like, but I wanted to be absolutely sure." One of her good friends, Raina Beck, owned Sugar and Spice, an adult boutique that carried gorgeous lingerie, high end sex toys, and other erotic novelty items.

Dean was well aware of that, too.

THE AWAKENING
(The Marriage Diaries, Volume 1)

# About the Authors

## Carly Phillips

Carly Phillips is the *N.Y. Times* and *USA Today* Best-selling Author of over 50 sexy contemporary romance novels featuring hot men, strong women and the emotionally compelling stories her readers have come to expect and love. Carly is happily married to her college sweetheart, the mother of two nearly adult daughters and three crazy dogs (two wheaten terriers and one mutant Havanese) who star on her Facebook Fan Page and website. Carly loves social media and is always around to interact with her readers. You can find out more about Carly at www.carlyphillips.com.

## Erika Wilde

Erika Wilde is the author of the sexy Marriage Diaries series and The Players Club series. She lives in Oregon with her husband and two daughters, and when she's not writing you can find her exploring the beautiful Pacific Northwest. For more information on her upcoming releases, please visit website at www. erikawilde.com.

CPSIA information can be obtained
at www.ICGtesting.com
Printed in the USA
LVOW13s2334071216
516327LV00006B/222/P